MW00929710

Bryan Chick
and Brett Radlicki

Andrews McMeel
PUBLISHING®

Table of Contents

Based on a true story.

No, really.

Chapter 1
Tommy Takes the Field

I'm Tommy Thompson, and almost everyone knows me by my fake fart sounds. The Wet Fart, the Slide Whistle, the Firecracker. I can make them with any body part. Armpits are for amateurs—I can make a fart noise with my *ears*. Here's me:

TERRY THOMAS THOMPSON ANGEL

I just finished fifth grade, and I'll be starting middle school in a few months. It's a time when kids split up into little packs: *the populars*, **THE ARTISTS**, THE GAMERS, the nerds. And the **Super Sports Society**, who rule the school and live like royalty.

To be in the Super Sports Society, you have to be amazing at a sport. Any sport, really, but emphasis on the **AMAZING** part. Brooke Meijers broke a record last year for how high her horse jumped; Leilani Akter is a gymnast who can hold her handstand for a whole forty-five minutes; and Brayton Ellis can lift a 120-pound weight over his head!

I *totally* see myself in the **Super Sports Society**.

I love baseball, and I've been playing for years. The only problem is I've been playing in a rec league, not a travel league. Everyone sees travel ballers as **BIG-TIME** serious:

and rec players as, well, a little more relaxed:

A lot of kids in the Super Sports Society are on travel teams. A bunch play baseball for the Bulldogs, who are a big deal in our small town of Wurtmore. Everyone goes to their games and fundraisers. I've wanted to be a Bulldog for as long as I can remember.

Wurtmore School District Photo Record

Kindergarten   1st Grade   2nd Grade

3rd Grade   4th Grade   5th Grade   6th Grade

PHOTO HERE

You can't play in their division until you're eleven, which I just turned. Being a Bulldog could set me up for middle school, for high school, for college—maybe even for **LIFE!**

The first day of tryouts are about to start, and the contenders are spread out along the infield, huddled in little groups.

As I imagine how perfect my life will be once I'm a Bulldog, someone near me says, **"HEY."** I turn and come face-to-face with my best friend, Pel.

"Dude," I say. **"What are you *doing* here?"** Explaining my confusion isn't necessary. Pel hates sports more than anything.

He rolls his eyes and takes a deep, exaggerated breath. "My mom's making me try out."

I try to say something, but the words get caught in my throat. Can Pel's mom be any more naive about life? You don't try out for a travel team when you're an amateur.

"This is the Bulldogs, bro."

Pel takes another deep breath. "I know."

"It's a travel team," I add.

"I know that too."

"You have to be *good* to make a travel team."

"Explain that to my mom," he says. "She told me I'm not spending my entire summer playing VIDEO GAMES."

I stare at Pel, not knowing what to say or think. Pel loves video games the same way I love baseball. He must play a hundred hours a day.

"She wants me to be a better role model for Miguel and Alejandra," Pel says.

He's talking about his younger brother and sister.

"There's only one opening on the team," I reply.

"Good," Pel says. "Hopefully I'll get cut early."

"BRING IT IN!" comes a booming voice. It's Coach Payne, the head coach of the Bulldogs. He looks like this on the right:

Pretty intense, huh?

Coach Decker, the assistant coach, isn't much different.

Travel coaches aren't like rec coaches. They live, breathe, and fart sports.

Once everyone's gathered around Coach Payne, he starts assigning players to positions, pointing to areas along the field with his bat.

"YOU! TAKE LEFT!" he says to me.

He means left field, of course. As I hurry to the spot, I recognize the players at third and short because we were in the same rec league. I nod, and they nod, but no one says a word because we're so nervous. Tryouts for the Bulldogs are an ego-bruising, **GUT-WRENCHING** experience.

Pel ends up with another kid in right field. Once everyone has their spots, Coach Payne stands near the plate and bats a ball around. The kid at second bobbles an easy grounder and recovers by throwing a pea to home. The kid at third flashes his leather on a diving stop near the line. The competition for the open spot is going to be **TOUGH!**

The bleachers are packed with parents. Ma's there, but Dad's traveling for work this week—a big *whew!* because he won't be around for everyone to notice what a nerd he is.

I recognize the seven Bulldogs helping with tryouts.

They're all members of the Super Sports Society, and most of them have really cool nicknames. Though they're not much older than me, I've never talked to any of them. Elites don't associate with regular people.

Coach Payne **WHACKS** the ball my way. I field it on two hops and breathe a sigh of relief when my nervous throw hits the cutoff instead of the bleachers. I glance over to see if Pel noticed. He didn't because he's staring into space, looking bored out of his brain. His pants hang low, revealing the bright red band of his underwear, and he has a haircut that went out of style about four hundred years ago. It's called a mullet.

"DUDE!" I say, hoping to get his attention in the game before he gets drilled by a line drive. **"DUDE!"**

He glances my way, then stares skyward again, returning to his thoughts. A small part of me wishes I could be like him. Tonight, Pel gets to go home and play video games and not worry about being cool, or making the Bulldogs, or being part of the **Super Sports Society**.

But I'm not like Pel. If I don't make the team, I could end up spending middle school—and maybe even forever—making fart sounds all alone.

As I continue to stare at my best friend, I can't help but wonder what he's thinking.

Chapter 2
Pel vs. Baseball

Baseball is the **WORST**. I'm just standing here, dodging gnats and wishing I'd put on some bug spray. It's the hottest part of the day in the hottest part of the year, and there isn't any shade in sight! This game is more about sweating and swatting bugs than anything else.

Coach Payne hits the ball high into the air, and some kid in the infield (I think that's what it's called) runs under it to make the catch. If a ball comes my way and I try to do the same thing, I'll probably end up with a few TEETH MISSING. Mom can blame herself for the dentist bill.

Gaming is so much better than sports. There's almost no sweating, and you can mute other players when you're tired of hearing them talk. You can **SPRINT** and **jump** and **run** without any effort. Plus, there's usually a cool drink, something sugary and sweet, nearby. If video games had been invented before sports, there wouldn't be any athletes. Aside from esports, of course.

Another ball **rockets** off the end of Coach Payne's bat. Some kid bobbles the ball, then hurls it at the player standing near second base. It all seems so pointless. And boring.

I think about how Mom tossed Dad's old baseball mitt at me before shoving me out the front door just moments ago. How is playing baseball supposed to make me a better role model for Miguel and Alejandra? And what's so wrong with spending a few hours gaming?

BZZZ. BZZZ. BZZZ.

A stupid gnat lands in my eye.

BZZZ. BZZZ. BZZZ. BZZZZZZ.

Another flies into my ear.

I swing my mitt to scare off the other bugs and accidentally **WHACK!** myself in the face. A few players in the infield stare at me.

I look at Tommy, my best friend. He's leaning forward with his hands near his knees, ready to field the ball should it come his way. I've never seen him looking so determined. He's wanted to be a Bulldog his entire life. And he's wanted to be popular even longer.

Something smells. Something smells *really* bad. I hold my nose up and sniff the air, trying to pinpoint the source of the odor. It seems to be coming from the woods just beyond center field. I peer in that direction and notice what looks like a large rectangular box just past the edge of the grass. It resembles a plastic refrigerator, or maybe an old-time phone booth. My heart sinks as I realize what it is. **THE TURD TANK**.

I step back, clutch my mitt to my chest, and try not to breathe the contaminated air. The putrid smell is coming from the old Turdle that has haunted Wurtmore Park for years.

Run, Pel! The thought is like a voice in my head, full of urgency and despair. It's like I'm being guided by a game tutorial or a side quest character. ***Run off this cursed field and never look back!***

I take a few steps and stop. If Mom finds out I quit tryouts, there's no telling how she might react.

Turdles are porta-potties, and they're sadly a big deal around here. Bob Dankworth, the guy who owns Turdles Ltd., is also the town mayor. You pretty much can't go anywhere in Wurtmore without running into a Turdle. **THE TURD TANK** is the only Turdle infamous enough to have a nickname, and it's the oldest, smelliest Turdle of them all.

"KID—GET THE BALL!"

It's Coach Payne's booming voice, and I realize he's talking to me when I spot a white sphere with red stitches resting near my feet. A baseball.

"Kid—let's go!"

I grab the ball with one hand and hurl it toward the infield. It soars HiGHER and farther than I ever would have expected, then bounces into the glove of the kid playing second base.

I notice Tommy noticing me. He's as stunned as I am by the strength of my throw.

"NICE ARM, KID!" Coach Payne calls out. It seems like a compliment.

I fake a smile even though the coach is too far away to see it and then turn my attention back to the Turd Tank. The smell seems worse than before, but I could be imagining it. I try not to think of what's causing the stench—the sludge in the ground beneath the toilet, generations of human waste. Rumor has it that people are too scared to clean the old porta-potty. It's there as a last resort, for when you *really* can't hold it, and I'm hoping I never find out just how gross it is.

The longest-recorded time someone has been inside the Turd Tank is two minutes and twelve seconds. That record holder is Roy Davis, a kid who played shortstop for Wurtmore High a few years ago. The moment is commemorated on the side of the Turd Tank.

"*LET'S SEE SOME EFFORT OUT THERE!*" Coach Payne calls out.

"REMEMBER—**TEN OF YOU WON'T BE HERE TOMORROW!"**

When I realize he's talking about the first round of cuts, an idea fills me with hope. I might not be able to *quit* tryouts, but if I can get cut today, I can be gaming tomorrow, and Mom won't have anything to complain about!

I bend my knees and lean forward, mimicking the stance of the other players. I wait, which is practically all you do in baseball, and breathe through my mouth to avoid smelling the Turd Tank. When Coach Payne whacks the ball my way again, I deliberately miss the catch. And when I chase after the ball, I intentionally trip over my own feet and **FACE-PLANT IN THE GRASS.**

"YOU ALL RIGHT, KID?" Coach Payne calls out.

I climb to my feet and hold my thumb in the air. Then I run for the ball and make myself fall again.

"KID?" Coach Payne hollers.

I get up and wave to let everyone know I'm okay. Then I scoop up the ball and throw it toward the infield, but not as hard as before and at an angle.

I notice Tommy noticing me again. He's standing with his hands on his hips and nodding. This is what he expected from me, the kid who's best at playing video games.

I miss the next ball that comes my way. And then **THE NEXT** and **THE NEXT**. At one point, I drop my mitt and pretend to have trouble putting it back on. At another point, I step on my own heel to lose my shoe. Everyone notices what's happening, and I can practically see Coach Payne crossing out my name on his candidate list.

Before long, Coach Payne yells at a few of us to get to the bench to practice hitting. I run for the infield, glad to put some distance between me and the Turd Tank, and feel pleased that my time with baseball is coming to a quick end. Tomorrow I'll be fighting zombies, storming enemy lines, and relaxing in the cool breeze of the air-conditioning. Tomorrow I'll be Pel again.

Chapter 3
Tommy Twice

"All right, ballplayers!" Coach Payne shouts. "Let's see what you can do with a bat!"

Diesel struts toward the plate in her catcher gear. She has black hair and brown eyes; the padded chest protector she's wearing is almost too big for her narrow frame. You wouldn't know it by looking at her, but Diesel's the toughest kid on the Bulldogs. That's why Coach Payne has her behind the plate, breathing dust and getting clipped by foul tips.

A bunch of us head for the dugout, which is really just a fenced-in bench.

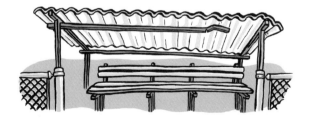

Sometimes rust drips down from the metal roof when it rains, but that's no big deal if you know the right spots to sit in.

On the bench, I squeeze in between Pel and some kid who could use a few swipes of deodorant. Caitlin Gupta, a girl with dark hair and rounded shoulders, is first at bat.

I elbow Pel to get his attention. **"What happened out there?"**

Pel turns to me with one eyebrow raised.

"In the outfield, bro," I add. **You missed every catch!"**

He shrugs one shoulder, as if showing he doesn't care. Good ol' Pel.

I lean in close to Pel and say, "Hey, I was just thinking about something."

"And what's that?" Pel asks, but not with a tone that suggests he really wants to know.

I lean in a little closer. "Most of the Bulldogs have nicknames."

"So?"

"So I'd fit right in with mine."

Pel studies me for a moment, which he's always doing and which is annoying. "You're talking about 'Tommy,' right?"

"Huh?"

"Your nickname," he says. "It's Tommy."

I roll my eyes. "I'm talking about my *other nickname*—the good one!"

Pel looks at me like I'm speaking Klingon. "You have another nickname?"

"**Tommy Twice**—*duh*."

"Who calls you that?"

"Pete!" Pete's the owner of Pete's Pickles, the party store in town. "He says it plays off the literature in my name."

"The what?"

"The literature."

"The alliteration, you mean."

"What*ever*." Leave it to Pel to miss the point. "Do something for me. Call me Tommy Twice when I'm up to bat."

"No chance, man."

"Why not?"

"Because it's cringey," Pel says. "I've never called you that in my life."

I consider ways to persuade him and find one I like. "What if I pay you?"

"With *what*? You already took an advance on your allowance!"

I'll probably wear this everywhere!

It's true; I was recently at the flea market with Ma and needed to make an important purchase.

CRAAACCCK!

The ball flies off Gupta's bat. Clutch, a Bulldog wearing jeans with shredded knees, dives to the ground. When she emerges from a cloud of dust, the baseball is nestled in her glove. She whips a throw to a Bulldog named Tower, the lanky first baseman who's at least a foot taller than the rest of the team. The throw comes in short, and Tower scoops it out of the dirt.

"Okay," I say to Pel. "You call me Tommy Twice, and I'll give you the gift card I have for Wurt-more Games."

Pel's interest is piqued. "What's it worth?"

"Thirty bucks."

This **was** true at one point, but the card now has a balance of two dollars and eighty-two cents. I can worry about this fact after Pel finds out.

Pel rolls his eyes. "Fine, whatever."

I smile, imagining "Tommy Twice" in an explosive 3D font, like the kind on a monster truck, maybe. Or one of those energy drinks Ma never lets me buy. I picture the name on my schoolbooks:

on my baseball bat:

and on a banner in the gym:

CRAAACCCK!

On the pitcher's mound, Torque, a Bulldog with cloudlike curly hair, snags a line drive out of the air.

"THAT'S WHAT I'M TALKIN' ABOUT!" Coach Payne says—or hollers, actually. Coach Payne doesn't have a soft voice, not even when he's standing right next to you.

A few more players take turns at the plate. Some kid hits a single, another kid strikes out, and Mina Ahmad, a girl from my fourth-grade class, pops up to first.

Finally, it's my turn. I step into the batter's box, dig a tiny trench for my back foot, and spit through my teeth, which is something I practice whenever I can.

Torque stands sideways and hides the ball in her mitt. She steps and throws, and the ball **WHAPS** against Diesel's padded glove.

"There you go!" Diesel says, pointing to Torque with her mitt. She lobs the ball back to the mound while I casually stand there, pretending I meant to take the pitch. The truth is I never even saw it. It's like the ball teleported from Torque's hand to Diesel's glove.

"LET'S GO, TOMMY TWICE!"

It's Pel, of course. I glance around the infield, hoping the Bulldogs heard him. It doesn't seem like they did.

Torque sends the next pitch. I swing harder than I need to, and the bat slips out of my hands and spins like the blade of a helicopter—

—almost taking off Coach Payne's head before smashing against the backstop.

"Oops."

Coach Payne looks ready to chew me out. Instead, he picks up the bat and carries it over. "I believe this is yours."

"Thanks, bro."

He blinks. "What did you just say?"

I realize my mistake. "Thanks, Coach."

"That's what I thought you said."

I cough to clear my throat, and Coach Payne walks away. Then I settle back into my stance.

"YOU GOT THIS, TWICE TOMMY!"

Pel, again, but this time he gets the nickname all wrong. He's gonna end up confusing people!

I swing and miss on the next pitch.

"Relax," Diesel says, lobbing the ball back to the mound. "Level your swing."

I miss the next few pitches. I have no clue what's wrong—I usually clobber these things! When the sixth pitch comes in high and tight, I can't get out of the way, and the ball hits my helmet like a **LIGHTNING BOLT**! I go down like a bag of bricks.

Diesel springs out of her catcher's squat and leans over me before I can get up. "Dude—you okay?"

It's possible, I guess. But given how hard Torque throws, it's also possible that my skull's in twenty pieces. In rec league, I never had to worry about being sent to the hospital because of a pitch.

Coach Payne's head appears in my view, blocking most of the blue sky. When I notice myself reflecting in both lenses of his sunglasses, all I can think is *Tommy Twice*.

He looks at Coach Decker and shouts, **"DECKER! WHAT'S THE CONCUSSION PROTOCOL?"**

Coach Decker stands on the sidelines, looking far too casual. "Beats me."

I'm surprised they don't just drag me off the field.

Coach Payne reaches into his back pocket and pulls out a handbook titled *Wurtmore Parks Youth Sport Manual.* He flips through the pages, saying, *"Concussions . . . concussions . . . concussions . . ."* He stops about halfway through the book and reads, "What's my name?"

"Coach Payne."

"What's *your* name?" he asks, after reading another line.

"Thompson," I say.

"What day is it?"

"Um . . . *Wednesday*?"

"Repeat these numbers backward: four, three, seven."

"Seven, four, three."

"Close enough."

He grabs my wrist and yanks me to my feet. "Take a seat for a few. If you don't puke or pass out, we'll get you back in the game."

I straighten my helmet and head to the dugout, trying not to notice how hard Goetz is laughing at me.

"SHAKE IT OFF, T TWICE!"

That's Pel, and he's switching up the nickname again to tease me. But *T Twice* is actually really cool. It sounds like an old-school rapper or something.

I drop to the bench beside Pel and take a deep breath.

"You okay?" Pel asks.

"I'm fine."

"You don't look—"

"Who's up?"

Coach Payne yells at the bench.

"That's me!" Pel says.

Twice Twice Baby!

Too cold... Too cold...

He jumps up and strips off my batting helmet, almost taking my ears with it. As he steps out of the dugout, I hope he won't be too embarrassed by what's about to happen.

Chapter 4
Pel at the Plate

I step in beside the plate, steady the oversize helmet with one hand, and bend my knees the way Tommy did. I have one thing in mind: **not hitting a single pitch**. It shouldn't be difficult. I haven't swung a bat in years, not since first grade when Tommy used to make me play in his backyard with a plastic bat.

Torque turns sideways on the mound. Her back foot touches the rubber, and she delivers her first pitch. The ball **WHAPS!** against Diesel's glove before I can even think about swinging. I'd spend a lifetime striking out in this league.

"Okay," Diesel says to me as she tosses the ball back to Torque. "You've seen one."

I nod, pretending to know what she means, and settle back into my stance. I deliberately stand too straight, rest the bat on my shoulder, and focus on what I'll be doing tomorrow, which is battling a bunch of pixel invaders from outer space.

Torque delivers the next pitch, and it blows right past me. It smacks against Diesel's glove in a tiny cloud of dust.

Someone chuckles on the bench, and I glance over to see that it's Tommy. He hides his smile when our gazes meet.

Diesel tosses the ball back to the mound. When the next pitch comes, it jets by me, and Tommy hides his smile again.

"**SERIOUSLY?**" I say under my breath, annoyed at Tommy. He doesn't have to love watching me fail this much.

"Huh?" Diesel says.

I shake my head. "Nothing."

Her gaze follows mine, and she seems to notice Tommy.

"Step out of the box," she says to me. She tosses the ball to Torque without rising out of her squat and adds, "Take a few practice swings."

I back away from the plate and swing a few times. The movement feels natural enough.

"Nice," she says. "Level it out and keep your eye on the ball."

I nod, having some idea of what she's talking about because I've played enough video games that feel the same way. As I step back to the plate, I overhear Tommy talking about me to the kid beside him on the bench.

"He shouldn't be out here," Tommy says. "He's never played a day of rec."

"FORGET HIM," Diesel says, which means she also heard Tommy. "Just keep your elbow up and swing through the pitch."

I lean forward and lift the bat off my shoulder. Something about the stance is strangely energizing. And exciting. A part of me **wants** to hit the ball—to show Tommy and Diesel and everyone else that I can.

"THERE YA GO!" Diesel says. She smacks her hand against her glove a couple times, and it almost seems like she's clapping—for *me*.

When the next pitch comes, I swing as hard as I can and manage to hit the bottom of it. The ball flies off at an angle and smacks against the backstop, rattling the fencing.

"THAT'S IT!" Diesel says. She grabs a new ball from a nearby bucket and tosses it to Torque. "Got a piece of it there!"

As I settle back into my stance, I glance at the bench. Tommy isn't grinning or talking trash. And he's paying more attention to me.

I connect a bit with the next pitch, and the ball rolls out of bounds before it gets to first base.

"Better," Diesel says. She tosses a new ball to Torque and adds, "Straighten it out."

I take a deep breath, settle in beside the plate, and look at the bench again. All the Bulldogs are now watching, and it feels weird that they could be interested in *me*, Pel. I'm the quiet kid. The gamer. The one who sits alone at lunch when Tommy isn't around.

Torque takes a deep breath while holding the ball in her mitt. Then she locks her gaze on Diesel's glove and delivers the next pitch. I keep my eye on the ball, swing the way Diesel described, and—

CRAAACCCK!

The ball jumps off my bat and soars out of the infield. It lands in the grass behind second base.

Tommy stares at me, and I stare at my bat.

"No way," I say under my breath.

"NICE SHOT!" Diesel says.

"Th-thanks."

Diesel smacks her hand against her mitt and says, "Let's see it again."

I nod and step back up to the plate. Then I bend my knees deeper than before and swing the end of my bat in a small circle. My body feels different—**strong** and ROOTED IN THE EARTH. When the next pitch comes, I hit another line drive, this one over the kid between second and third base.

"You blistered that one!" Diesel says. "Left-center gap."

It's a different language—the language the Bulldogs speak. A part of me wonders what it would feel like to know a few words.

"Isn't that your friend?" I overhear someone on the bench ask Tommy.

Tommy nods, gazing into the outfield.

"What's his name?" the kid asks.

"Pel," Tommy says.

"What kind of name is that?"

Tommy shrugs one shoulder and watches the throw come in. "A nickname."

"His nickname's Pel?"

"His nickname's Pelican, actually," Tommy says. "But everyone calls him Pel."

"A nickname of a nickname," the kid says, grinning. **"SWEET."**

I roll the tension out of my shoulders and step up to the plate again. When the next pitch comes, I send it into right field.

"THAT'S HOW WE DO!" Coach Payne shouts.

The kids on the bench are nudging one another and pointing. I can't tell if they're excited or intimidated by how good I'm hitting.

"What's your real name?" Diesel asks me. She must have overheard the conversation on the bench too.

I shrug, feeling embarrassed for some reason. "I'm just Pel."

It's true. I've been Pel since forever.

I hit five of the next eight pitches. When Coach Decker asks for the next batter, I fist-bump Diesel and head back to the bench with a little swagger in my step.

I get a few high fives while walking through the dugout, then I plop down on the bench beside Tommy. "Well?"

"Well what?" Tommy says.

"How did I do?" I ask.

He shrugs one shoulder. "Pretty good, I guess."

"You guess?"

He nods ever so slightly. "But 'pretty good' doesn't mean you're ready for the Bulldogs."

In Tommy's world, it's sort of a compliment.

Once everyone has a chance to bat, we break up into groups to run a few drills, and for some reason, I find myself doing my best. At the end of the afternoon, Coach Payne tells us to grab our gear and meet him on the field. As he summarizes our play, the Bulldogs pass around a bag of ranch-flavored sunflower seeds. Pits shoves a handful into his mouth and starts working his jaw like a cow chewing cud. After a few seconds, he spits a bunch of cracked shells all around.

"A lot of you were late on your swings," Coach Payne says. "But that's typical for kids coming up from rec."

Tower grabs the bag and loads up on a bunch. When it's Diesel's turn, she pours some right into her mouth, which is especially impressive because she's still wearing her catcher's mask. Cracked seeds fly like fireworks, and the whole spectacle is pretty awesome.

Coach Payne steps up and grabs the bag of sunflower seeds. He dumps some into his mouth and starts cracking them while he talks. Shells fly everywhere, seemingly propelled by his words. "**Props to Pel!** He had some nice hits today."

I feel my cheeks flush, and I'm not sure what to think. I look at Tommy, at Diesel, and then at my feet.

"That's all I got!" Coach Payne adds. "Your parents will get an email tonight letting 'em know if you made **the first cut**."

Most of the kids and both coaches disperse. Tommy and I stare at the shells of the sunflower seeds. They look like confetti.

"Who has sunflower seeds as a snack?" I ask.

"Anyone who's serious about baseball," Tommy says. His eyes jump up and land on me. "What are you doing tonight?"

"I'll probably get started on some summer reading." It's a joke, of course. We both know what **"SUMMER READING"** means.

"Do you have your bike?" Tommy asks.

I nod. Though Wurtmore's not the most exciting town in the world, it's probably the safest. A lot of middle school—aged kids ride their bikes without supervision, at least during the day when the weather is good. The streets have sidewalks and pedestrian crossings. And drivers know to be on the lookout for kids on their bikes.

"Good," Tommy says. "I need your help."

"With what?"

He lowers his eyebrows and gets really serious.

"MAKING THE TEAM."

Before I can ask another question, he turns and heads for his bike. I follow him for some reason, wondering what I'm getting myself into now.

Chapter 5
Pete's Pickles

Pel and I lean our bikes against the brick wall of Pete's Pickles. The owner of the store, Pete, has been around for a **thousand years**, and he'll tell you stories about the days when Wurtmore was just a grassy plain with a spatter of people.

WURTMORE
Population 147
(livestock included)

   Back then, Pete ran a pickle stand at carnivals and fairs. His pickles became sort of a **BIG DEAL**, and over time, that pickle stand became a pickle shop. That pickle shop went on to become a party store, Wurtmore's one-stop shop for chips, dips, and sugary drinks. These days, it's even a small grocery. But Pete's still into pickling. His front counter is lined with giant pickle jars. Each pickle costs two bucks and is about the size of a small watermelon.

The store sign reads "Pete's Pickles" in separate blue letters that light up at night. As for the apos-

trophe, it's a pickle, and that's a nice touch.

A few years ago, the **s** in **Pickles** fell off and broke. Everyone had a good laugh about that. Except Pete. It took him weeks to get a replacement letter, and by that time, photos of his sign were all over the Internet. It didn't take long for the memes to start showing up.

"Are you gonna tell me what we're doing?" Pel asks.

I take off my helmet, throw on my ballcap, and head for the entrance with my backpack still on and my cleats clicking on the concrete. I shoulder open the door, lead Pel down the aisle filled with candy and chips, and find what I'm looking for.

"Sunflower seeds?" Pel asks.

"You saw the Bulldogs, right?"

Pel has that look on his face like he can't believe what he's hearing.

"Don't you get it?" I add. "Travel coaches want players who fit the mold."

"And let me guess," Pel says. "That mold includes not only having a nickname but also being able to spit sunflower seeds."

"You're catching on." The seeds come in a bunch of varieties like ranch, salt and vinegar, sizzling bacon, and more. Which ones will make me look like a **FUN, THRILL-SEEKING FUTURE MEMBER** of the

Super Sports Society? I pull a bag off a hook and hand it to Pel. "Here."

Pel reads the label. "Why would I want to eat a seed that tastes like a taco?"

"Exactly." I hand him a few more bags. "These too."

"Low sodium?"

"TO TRAIN WITH."

"Train with?" Pel says. "And how are you gonna pay for all this?"

I wink to show I know what I'm doing. We walk to the front of the store, where Pete is standing behind a long line of pickle jars.

"Uh-oh,"Pete says. "Here comes trouble."

Pel and I drop everything on the counter.

"You boys going into quarantine?"

"Baseball," I say.

"I figured you just played video games."

"In a perfect world," Pel quips.

Pete starts ringing up the items. "I played ball as a kid, you know. Back when Wurtmore was just a grassy plain. Those gnats are the worst!"

Pel practically jumps out of his cleats. "I know, *right*?"

"I wasn't much on the field—but, boy, was I good with the lumber."

"The lumber?" Pel asks.

I roll my eyes. "The *bat*."

"Me too!" Pel says to Pete. "I had the farthest hit today!"

"Bravo!" Pete's always using that word. It probably meant "cool" or "awesome" back in the days of grassy plains.

"*Maybe* it was the farthest hit," I say. "It's not like we measured it or anything."

Pel gives me a look, and Pete ignores me.

"Pel—how about a PiCKLE ON THE HOUSE?" Pete grabs a pair of tongs hanging behind him and adds, "Which flavor?"

Pel eyes the pickles for so long that I'm pretty sure we'll be biking home in the dark.

"Dill," he says at last.

"Oh, a *classic!*" Pete unscrews the lid and uses the tongs to grab a pickle. He wraps it in tin foil, hands it Pel, then turns to me and says, "How about you, Tommy Twice? Care for a pickle?"

"Sure." I play it off like being offered a pickle doesn't matter, but I've been longing to try the jalapeño flavor.

Pete must have a sixth sense or something, because he unscrews the lid on a new jar and hands over a jalapeño-flavored pickle. I take a bite, and it's all-caps **AWESOME!!**

Pete closes the jars and hangs up the tongs. Then he pushes some buttons on the register and says, "That'll be thirty-seven dollars and twelve cents."

My jaw drops. "For sunflower seeds?"

"For twelve bags, yeah."

"Just put it on my mom's tab."

Pete's eyebrow curves upward. "I usually put milk and bread on your mom's tab. You sure she sent you up here for *twelve bags* of sunflower seeds?"

I nod. "I don't question Ma."

"Hmm," Pete says. "I only ask because sunflower seeds are popular with baseball players."

"Really?" I say. "I never knew that."

Pete eyes me long enough for things to get uncomfortable. Then he puts the seeds in a grocery bag and holds it out to me. "I'll go ahead and put it on her tab. But I'll be sure to talk to your mother the next time she's in."

"Thanks, bro." I stuff the bag in my backpack. "And thanks for the pickle!"

"Arrivederci!" Pete's always saying goodbye in different languages. I'm pretty sure "arrivederci" is Italian.

Pel and I smile, step outside, and hurry up the sidewalk. We strap on our helmets and mount our bikes.

"Your house or mine?" I ask Pel.

"I'm going home," he says. "By *myself.*"

"Seriously?"

He crunches down on his boring dill pickle. "It's summer vacation, man. I've been awake almost six hours without playing a video game. Do you have any idea how *wrong* that is?"

"But what if I need help?"

"With what? Opening the bags?"

"Technique or something," I explain. "You think it's easy spitting shells the way Diesel does?"

"I'm not—" Pel starts.

"*C'mon,* bro—you can play games later!"

Pel thinks about it. Then he takes another bite of his pickle and says, "A half hour, dude, **THAT'S IT**. Then I'm gaming."

I smile, adjust my backpack, and head for Pel's house. I'm nearly certain I'll be a Bulldog and a fully fledged member of the Super Sports Society in a few days' time.

Chapter 6
Seeds of Change

"Hmm." I hold up a sunflower seed like an antique dealer inspecting an old coin. "Seems like a choking hazard."

Tommy rolls his eyes and continues to click through the Internet search results for **"HOW TO SPIT SUNFLOWER SEEDS LIKE A PRO."** Apparently, you're supposed to crack each one in half with your teeth and use your tongue to dig out the kernel. Then you spit out the busted shell.

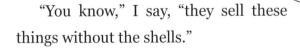

"You know," I say, "they sell these things without the shells."

"And the point of that would be . . . ?"

We're sitting on an old porch swing at my house. Mom is inside on a video conference call.

Tommy skims through the search results once more, sets his phone in his lap, and pops a seed into his mouth. He moves his jaw UP, DOWN, LEFT, RIGHT. He squints one eye and then the other.

"You okay?" I ask.

He nods because his tongue is busy doing other things. When he spits out the shell, it's in a dozen pieces, most of which don't fly far.

"Shouldn't you already be good at this?" I ask.

"Sunflower seeds weren't really a thing in rec league." He plants a second seed in his mouth, works his jaw all around, and makes a mess with the shell pieces again. "Dude, this is harder than it looks. **You try.**"

I stare at my seed again. "This isn't the kind that tastes like a taco, is it?"

"Of course not," Tommy says. "We're saving those for when it's important."

I toss the seed in my mouth, crack it in half, and spit the pieces about three feet past the porch rail.

"Not bad," Tommy says.

I shrug. It doesn't feel like something I should be proud of.

"Okay—I'm going again." He takes a deep breath, focuses, and tosses another seed into his mouth. He moves his jaw a bunch of ways and then spits out a few pieces that dribble down his chin. "How was that?"

"Disgusting," I say. "And speaking of disgusting—does the Turd Tank always smell so bad?"

Tommy nods and tosses another seed in his mouth.

"Have you ever been inside?"

"No way!" His jaw shifts left and right as he works on the seed. "I have nightmares about that place—*real* nightmares."

I try not to think of what those nightmares might contain. "Does anyone use it?"

He spits out the pieces of the seed, which barely clear his shirt. "I hope not."

"But what if you have to go?"

"Then you hold it," Tommy says. "Or find a bush and hope no one records you on their phone."

The idea is just as terrifying as the Turd Tank.

While Tommy keeps practicing, I get in on the action too—not because I care about how far I can spit shells but because the seeds actually taste pretty good. Before we know it, we're out of low sodium and have to switch to sizzling bacon. Halfway through that bag, we have a couple visitors—

—but they head for the trees when Mom makes a loud noise in the house.

Tommy hands me his phone and says, **"RECORD ME."**

"Why?"

"I want to check my form."

I roll my eyes, hold up the phone, and start recording. Tommy spits out the next shell, which barely clears the porch rail.

"DUDE!" he shouts. "I gotta see that!"

I tilt the phone and hit *play.*

"*AWESOME*!" he says. "Send that to Pits!"

I look up at him, surprised. "You have his number?"

"Why wouldn't I?"

I can think of a couple good reasons. They're not friends, for one. And as far as I know, they've never talked. But when I go into Tommy's contacts, I find Pits's info.

Tommy must have over-heard someone giving out the number. Or maybe he found it on the school's internal website. Who knows.

"Did you send it?" Tommy asks.

I tap a few buttons and delete the recording while pretending to send it because Pits would never understand why Tommy sent him a video. I've been doing secret favors for Tommy all his life. Like the time I stopped him from throwing a snowball at the traffic guard directing cars at the Winter in Wurtmore parade. And the time I prevented him from jumping off a roof with a patio umbrella because he saw some action hero do it in a movie.

Just as we finish the bag of sizzling bacon, Tommy gets a text from his mother saying that he needs to go home. We kick the shells into the bushes and put the remaining bags of sunflower seeds in Tommy's backpack. Tommy mounts his bike and turns to me, looking nervous about something.

"What's wrong?" I ask.

"Nothing."

"C'mon, tell me."

"What if . . ." He stares into the distance as if looking for the right words. "What if you make the team and I don't?"

I shake my head. "Not gonna happen."

"It might," Tommy says. "You had a few good hits today."

"If it does happen, I'll forfeit the spot. My middle school plans don't include standing in a field, sweating."

"Mine do," Tommy says with a smile. "Seems weird, right?"

"Not really. You've wanted to be a Bulldog all your life."

"Everyone loves them."

It's true, at least in Wurtmore. Their games are always packed, and people party at their special events—like the Bulldog Brawl, on the last day of tryouts. People treat it like Mardi Gras or something.

"Baseball defines me," Tommy says. "Is that a bad thing?"

"At least it puts you in the dictionary."

Tommy scrunches up his face. "Huh?"

"Nothing defines me," I explain.

"What about gaming?"

"Big deal."

"The way you play, it's *totally* a big deal. You're like a pro gamer, bro—only you still live at home and you don't have a sponsor."

I crack up. The best thing about Tommy is the way he makes me laugh.

Tommy checks the time on his phone and says, "I gotta bounce." He jumps up on the pedals and rides across the yard, adding, "Later, bro."

"Later, *T Twice!*"

Tommy shows me he likes the nickname and turns onto the street to head for whatever news is waiting for him at home. I hope it's good. He'll be **crushed** if I make it through first cuts and he doesn't.

The idea makes me nervous. The last thing I want is for something like baseball to get in the way of our friendship.

As I watch Tommy ride off, I think about playing on the ball field today. I remember standing at home plate, feeling so rooted in the earth, and listening to Diesel's encouragement. The Bulldogs were more friendly than I imagined they'd be.

Maybe forfeiting the spot wouldn't be so easy.

Chapter 7
Coach Payne's Email

I sit at the computer and stare at the blank screen. Coach Payne's email is likely a few clicks away.

"Ma!"

"Yeah?" Ma's in the kitchen, banging dishes around in the sink.

"I'm checking your email, okay?"

"I can't hear you!" she shouts over the noise she's making.

"I'M CHECKING YOUR EMAIL!"

"FINE, TOMMY!"

I hold my hand above the mouse. It's scary to think I'm so close to an extreme mood change. "UNLESS YOU WANT TO!"

"I CAN'T HEAR YOU, THOMAS! I'M DOING THE DISHES!"

Ma is *always* doing the dishes. Sometimes, I almost feel bad enough to help.

I look at the mouse like I'm waiting for it to come alive and bite off my fingers. When it doesn't, I give the smooth piece of plastic a little shake. The screen wakes up.

"What's your password?" I shout.

"TOMMY, I CAN'T HEAR—"

"WHAT'S YOUR PASSWORD?"

Dorothy Thompson

Password

The dishes stop banging around in the sink, and then my mother steps into the room holding a sudsy plate. "Rescueme," she says. "One word, capital *R*."

"Seriously?"

She raises an eyebrow. "*Seriously.*"

"What do you need to be rescued from?"

"Oh . . . nothing, honey."

I type in "Rescueme" with a capital *R* and find a new email in the inbox. It's from Coach Payne. I close my eyes so I don't accidentally read something.

"Well?" Ma says, still standing just inside the doorway. "What does it say?"

I slowly open one eye. The subject line reads **Tryouts: Day 1.**

"Tommy, what does—"

"Hold on!"

I hover the pointer over the email. Then I work up the courage to double-click.

Dear Parent,

THOMAS THOMPSON is invited to participate in day two of the four-day tryouts for the Bulldogs. Please make sure **THOMAS THOMPSON** is at Wurtmore Park tomorrow at 1:00. I look forward to seeing **THOMAS THOMPSON.**

Sincerely,

Coach Payne

I read the email a second time, a third, a fourth. When I realize I'm not seeing things, I jump up and do a few celebration dances that Pel and I have been practicing—the dances you see in sports and video games.

"I'm guessing you made it?" Ma says.

I continue to dance, vaguely aware that the floor is shaking.

Ma walks over and kisses the top of my head. "Great job, kid." She smiles, then turns and leaves the room, leaving a trail of soap suds.

I grab my phone and text Pel.

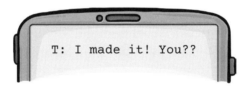

T: I made it! You??

I stare at the screen, eager for Pel's response. It comes within seconds.

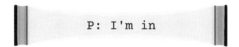

P: I'm in

I start to type *Sweet!* but can't bring myself to do it.

It isn't sweet. There's only one spot on the team, and Pel is the competition.

I search my thoughts for a different response and finally find something.

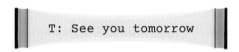

T: See you tomorrow

Pel doesn't respond right away, as if he's considering what to type. Then his response finally appears on the screen.

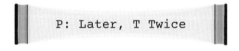

P: Later, T Twice

Something about his words make me nervous.

Chapter 8
Is Pel Cut Out for This?

I stare at my phone, feeling uneasy.

Footsteps sound in the hall, and Mom appears in the doorway to the home office, where I'm seated at the desk. Her dark hair is pulled back.

"WELL?" she asks.

I know what she's asking because I've been checking her email (with permission) every ten minutes for the past two hours. I glance at the computer screen, which is still displaying Coach Payne's email.

"I made it," I say.

Her eyes light up. "You did?"

"It's just the first round of cuts," I explain before she can get too excited. "There are three more rounds and—"

Before I can finish, she races across the room and plants a kiss on top of my head.

"See?" she says. "I knew you'd be good—just like your father."

My heart sinks in my chest a bit. It's never easy talking about Dad.

"Did you tell Miguel and Alejandra?" Mom asks.

"Not yet."

She kisses me again and runs from the room, calling out the names of my younger siblings.

Happy to see Mom so excited, I read Coach Payne's email again. Never in a million years would I have expected to make the first round of cuts for an opening on Wurtmore's cherished baseball team.

I stare out the window and think about the day—the baseballs I hit and the good throw I made. I picture Diesel in her catcher's stance, her glove held forward, waiting for the pitch. She was nice to me, and so were the other Bulldogs, which wasn't something I expected. And Coach Payne was full of compliments. I always figured he just yelled at his team.

"Pel?" The soft voice pulls me out of my thoughts, and I look across the room to see my five-year-old sister, Alejandra. She's standing in the doorway, wearing her baseball cap and glove.

"Hey, Ale," I say.

"Wanna play catch?" she asks.

I smile. Mom must have already told her all the good news.

"Sure," I say.

Her face comes alive with excitement, then she turns and runs down the hall. I listen to the fade of her footsteps. And I continue smiling as the door to the backyard slams open and shut.

I rise from the chair. When I realize I'm still holding my phone, I glance down and see my last text to Tommy again.

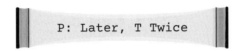

P: Later, T Twice

Why do I feel **weird** about this?

I drop my phone on the desk, anxious to get it out of my hands. Then I leave the room, make my way down the hall, and grab my mitt off the couch.

When I push out the back door, a part of me imagines I'm stepping onto the field at Wurtmore Park in a Bulldogs jersey.

Chapter 9
Big Ray's

The next morning before tryouts, Ma drives me and Pel to Big Ray's, a sporting goods store just outside Wurtmore. I'm in the passenger seat, which I just graduated to after a growth spurt, and Pel's in the back. Last night, Coach Payne sent a second email stating that athletic cups are mandatory for us. Pel doesn't have one, and I outgrew mine last season.

"I wish you'd stop doing that," Ma says. "It's **disgusting**." She's talking about my new seed-spitting habit. I've nearly gone through a bag of honey mustard since leaving the house fifteen minutes ago. "You're gonna miss the window."

"I'm *not* gonna miss the window." I spit another shell outside to show off my accuracy.

Ma looks at Pel through the rearview mirror. "I didn't know you liked baseball, Pel."

Pel shrugs one shoulder. "I thought I'd try it."

It's a lie, of course, because Pel's mom is making him play.

"Well," she says, "I hope you have fun."

"It'll be tough for him to make the team," I point out. "He never played rec."

"I'm sure he'll do just *fine,* Tommy." Ma hangs a right turn into a mall complex. "I'm *totally* looking forward to the Bulldog Brawl this week! It's always such a party. It's the last day of tryouts, right?"

"Yup, Saturday," I say, a little worried I might not be there for it. Only the kids who make it to the end of tryouts get to participate. "Aww, *c'mon!*"

"What's wrong?" Ma says.

I turn my bag of sunflower seeds upside down to show her. "I'm out—and that was **the last bag!**"

"You ate everything?" Pel says.

"You know," Ma says, "you're gonna upset your stomach if you keep eating those things."

"They're seeds, Ma. Not pizza rolls."

"Birds eat seeds," Ma says as she turns into the parking lot of Big Ray's. "Have you ever seen their poop?"

"Yep, and it looks nothing like mine."

She pulls into a spot and stops the engine. **"You boys sure you don't want me to go in with you?"**

"We're good."

Shopping for an athletic cup is embarrassing enough without your mom tagging along. Everyone knows the body part they're meant to protect. Besides, if Mom hangs back, she can listen to her oldies on the radio.

Pel and I exit the car and drag our feet on our way to the entrance.

"I'm not ready for this," Pel says.

"Don't *worry*," I say. "We use the self-checkout line, and no one sees a thing."

Pel glances at me like he isn't convinced.

The automatic doors yawn open, and we step inside. Big Ray's is roughly the size of Rhode Island and smells like a tennis ball. We pull our ball caps as low as they'll go and start checking the aisles.

"Can I help you?" a voice says.

I jump backward, bumping into Pel and almost knocking him over. A teenage girl is standing in front of us.

"Are you looking for something specific?"

I try to answer, but the words get stuck in my throat. Pel just blushes.

The girl grins. "Athletic cups are in aisle fifteen." She walks off to save us from any more embarrassment.

"LET'S MOVE!" I whisper-scream at Pel.

We crouch low and hustle toward aisle fifteen like soldiers behind enemy lines. When I spot Mrs. Pereira, our third-grade teacher, we duck into aisle

eleven, pretending to be interested in badminton, which, of course, no one is.

Once Mrs. Pereira goes whistling by, we slink back out into the main aisle, pressing on.

Big buckets of bubble gum are stacked on the endcap of aisle thirteen.

"Dude," I say, "this is a *seriously* good price!"

"We're not here for bubble gum."

"The big leaguers are always chewing this stuff," I say. "It's usually too expensive to buy."

"And it still is. You have no money, remember?"

"Sure I do." I grab a bucket. "Ma gave me some."

"Yeah, for a cup."

"I'll just get a cheaper one."

Pel stares at me like he can't believe what I said. "Maybe an off-brand cup isn't the best idea for something that's supposed to protect your—"

"**DUDE—CHILLAX.**" "Chillax" is, like, my favorite word, and I'm always happy for a chance to use it. "I know what I'm doing."

We make it to aisle fifteen and stand there, checking over our shoulders. When we're sure no one's watching, we duck down the aisle, ready for anything. The cups are hanging from hooks on a pegboard. They come in different shapes and sizes—not just the waistband but the important part.

"What now?" I ask.

"Pull one down and read the label."

"Why don't *you* pull one down?"

"Baseball's your thing, remember?"

I put down the bucket of bubble gum and turn to Pel with my fist planted against the palm of my other hand. **"Rock paper scissors."**

"Fair enough," Pel says, striking the same pose. We've been using rock paper scissors to settle disputes for as long as I can remember.

"Best of three," Pel says. "And I count."

"You are *so* toast!"

We stare into each other's eyes to make sure there's no cheating. Then Pel starts the count:

"Rock...
paper...
scissors...
SHOOT!"

I go with rock and can't believe when Pel counters with paper. Pel celebrates with one of the dances we've been practicing.

"It's best of *three*!" I say, holding my starting position again.

"Fine." Pel places his fist on his palm and starts the count:

"Rock . . .
paper . . .
scissors . . .
SHOOT!"

I come back with scissors and get smoked again. It's like Pel can read my mind!

"Whatever, bro," I say. "I'll do it since you're such a **WIMP**!"

I pause to see if Pel will take the bait and prove he's tough. It doesn't happen.

I glance over both shoulders to make sure the teenager from the front of the store isn't around. Then I reach out and pull down the nearest cup.

Chapter 10
Cup Holders

Standing in aisle fifteen, looking embarrassed out of his mind, Tommy turns the box over and reads the description on the back.

"Well?" I ask.

"This one's made with '**polymers**,'" Tommy says. "That mean anything to you?"

"Not at all."

Tommy glances around to make sure the coast is clear and reads some more. "It's supposed to **SHIELD** and **transfer** shock away from the groin."

"That seems important," I say.

"And it has a gel pad to prevent chafing."

"What's chafing?"

"I don't know," Tommy says. "Look it up on the Internet, bro."

I do and read the search results: "'An irritation which occurs when skin rubs against itself or an external object like clothing.'"

"Well, that's horrifying." Tommy hangs the cup back up, grabs another one, and reads the label. "Peewee—this one should work for you, since you've got PEEWEE SKILLS as a player." He chuckles at his own joke and tosses the box at me. I dodge the box instead of catch it, and the cup slides out when the box hits the floor.

"Dude—pick it up!" Tommy says, checking over his shoulders.

"No chance, man," I say. "**YOU** pick it up!"

"No way! **YOU**!"

"**YOU!**"

"Rock paper scissors," Tommy says, resting his fist on his palm again. "One shot."

It's the right choice to save time. I position my hands like Tommy's and then handle the count: **"Rock . . . paper . . . scissors . . . SHOOT!"**

Tommy goes with rock, and I smoke him again. To celebrate, I cycle through a few dances: **the Hype**, **the Tidy**, and **the Lunar Party**.

"Fine!" Tommy says.

Tommy picks up the cup and holds it out for us to see. It's just a curvy piece of plastic, really.

"What do you think the holes are for?" I ask.

"Ventilation?"

An idea seems to strike Tommy; he glances over his shoulder to check for people again. He holds the cup up to his face, covering his nose and mouth like a mask. Then, in a Darth Vader voice, he says—

"Dude—are you nuts?" I say. Our lives will be **OVER** if someone from Wurtmore Middle School walks over and sees us. But Tommy knows that the best jokes often involve extreme risk-taking, and I can't help but crack up.

When three people suddenly walk up the aisle behind Tommy, I stop laughing and my cheeks redden. It's Diesel, Goetz, and Alfredo. Diesel looks mortified, but Goetz and Alfredo are grinning from ear to ear. To my horror, Tommy doesn't notice them.

Tommy starts making fart sounds that get amplified by the cup. The **WIPE OUT**, the **Ripper**, the **PULL OVER!** I know their names because I've heard the sounds for years.

"Dude—no," I whisper as the Bulldogs continue to close in behind him.

"Don't stop me now," he says. "I'm just getting *farted*."

He laughs and continues with more fart sounds. The **Predator**, the **FiZZLE**, and then the **ACCIDENTAL SPLAT**.

"Um . . . what are you guys *doing*?" comes a voice. It's Diesel. She and the other Bulldogs walk up and stop beside Tommy.

Tommy turns his head, still holding the cup to his face. His eyes widen when he sees the three Bulldogs. As he lowers his arms, I throw together a mental list of possible explanations. It looks like this:

Possible Explanations
1
2
3
4
5
6
7
8
9
10

Tommy is clearly too horrified to speak.

"We were . . ." I keep reviewing the mental list, hoping something will appear. "We were just . . . you know . . ."

Goetz aims his gaze at Tommy like a weapon. "I think that's supposed to go somewhere else."

Tommy just stands there, holding the cup to his face. I cry on the inside while pretending to laugh. Then I put together a mental list of really cool comebacks. It looks like this:

Tommy blushes. His eyes shift **LEFT**, *RIGHT,* and then he hides the cup behind his back. When his eyes widen even more, I realize something's very wrong.

"You all right?" Diesel asks.

Tommy turns his body so the Bulldogs can't see behind him, and I get a clear view of the problem.

Tommy reaches back with his free hand and twists and pulls on the cup. His pinky doesn't budge.

"Ummm," Diesel says. "Did you get your finger stuck in that cup?"

Tommy tries to play it cool. "What cup?"

"The one that was on your face."

"Oh, *that* cup."

He pulls as hard as he can and his finger **POPS** out. The cup **SHOOTS** across the aisle and lands in the web of a nearby baseball glove, like a perfect catch.

Goetz and Alfredo start cracking up. Diesel continues to look disturbed.

Tommy keeps playing it cool. He glances at his hand and smiles to show how perfect everything is.

"What's your name again?" Diesel asks.

"Everyone calls him *TOMMY TWICE*," I say. I realize too late that it was the wrong time to drop the nickname.

"This kid's weird," Goetz says, looking over at Tommy. "We don't need weird kids in the Bulldogs. It'll make us look bad to the whole Super Sports Society."

Tommy's cheeks redden, and I know he'd like nothing more than to disappear.

Diesel turns to her friends. "C'mon, guys—let's find the batting gloves."

She walks off with Alfredo, but Goetz just stands there, grinning. He picks up the empty box and laughs at the description. Then he throws the box to Tommy and says, "Stick to rec ball, Fart Face. You'll never make it on a travel team."

I stand there feeling **smaller** than ever in the huge sports store. Tommy takes a step forward, as if to defend himself. But because he's Tommy and I'm Pel, Goetz can do whatever he wants.

"Guten Tag," Goetz says, speaking German. He turns and walks off, looking pleased by how miserable he can make us.

"Forget about him, man," I say to Tommy. "He doesn't matter."

But it isn't true. He does matter. If Goetz doesn't like Tommy, none of the Bulldogs will.

Chapter 11
Back at Pete's

"What about this one?" I ask, holding up a bag of zesty ranch. After Big Ray's, Ma drove us home. Pel and I met up on our bikes and headed to Pete's Pickles just before tryouts.

"Works for me," Pel says.

I roll my shoulders to adjust my backpack and sort through the other flavors of sunflower seeds.

Which one says the most about my personality?

Which one can make Diesel, Goetz, and Alfredo forget about what they just saw?

"You boys need some help?" Pete asks. He's standing behind the front counter, stirring a jar of pickles with a spoon.

"We're good!" I feel a pinch in the seat of my baseball pants and make an adjustment—a poke here, a pull there.

"What was **THAT**?" Pel asks.

"What was **WHAT**?" I make another adjustment, this time to my front.

"Are you already wearing your cup?"

"Of course. I'm breaking it in." Another pinch, another pull. "Like running shoes."

Pel laughs, and I throw a bag of buffalo-style ranch at him to keep him quiet. Then I decide on a few bags of BBQ and head to the front of the store.

"More seeds?" Pete asks as I drop everything on the counter.

"Yep."

He rings up the order. "You're gonna upset your stomach, you know."

"Huh?"

"All these seeds—they're loaded with fiber." He continues tapping his fingertips along the register. "Fiber makes you poop."

I roll my eyes, thinking about how much he sounds like Ma. Old people must spend half their day worried about bathroom stuff. My grandma is always eating prunes, and Dad won't go near a cup of coffee unless he's three steps away from a toilet.

"Twenty-eight dollars and twelve cents," Pete says.

"Go ahead and put it on my mom's tab," I reply.

"Again?"

"Yeah, it's no biggie. She'll just take it out of my allowance."

Pete raises an eyebrow. "That must be quite an allowance."

"I do *a lot* of work around the house." It might be the biggest lie of my life.

Pete hands over the bags. "Okay, but I still plan on talking to your mother when I see her."

I grab the sunflower seeds. "No problem." It's actually a **BIG PROBLEM**, but not at the moment, which is all that matters.

Pel and I head to tryouts.

Chapter 12
Get a Whiff of This

I step into the batter's box. That's when I hear a voice.

It isn't Obi-Wan, and the voice isn't in my head. It's Diesel, squatting behind the plate in her catcher's gear. Through the mask, I see her devious grin. She's probably still laughing about what she saw in Big Ray's.

"Let's see what your bat's got today," she says.

She holds up her glove as a target, and Torque delivers the first pitch. I swing late, and the ball **WHAPS** against Diesel's glove.

"Little tardy on that one," she says, lobbing the ball back to the mound.

What she doesn't know is I meant to be.

I cock my elbow and wait for the next pitch. When it comes, I whiff again.

Coach Payne and Coach Decker haven't taken their eyes off me since I stepped up to the plate. Same with the players on the bench—especially Tommy. Everyone wants to see if I can hit as good as I did yesterday.

Another pitch, another miss. I step back and take a deep breath, pretending to be nervous when I'm actually perfectly fine. I remind myself that this is what I came here to do. Tommy needs the Bull-dogs, not me.

"Keep your head up!" says Coach Payne.

I get ready again. Torque sends one right down the middle, and I let it go by.

"C'mon!" Diesel says to me. "That was a meatball."

"Hey, Pel!" Goetz calls out from the bench. "You want me to bring out the tee?"

"Watch your mouth, Goetz!" Coach Payne hollers. "Or you're gonna be running!"

I stare at the mound, wondering what I could do with the next pitch if I tried. Part of me wants to show Coach Payne that he was right to defend me—to prove I'm good enough to be in the Bulldogs and stand in the spotlight for a change.

But I have Tommy to think about, so I swing and miss, *AGAIN* and **AGAIN**. Coach Payne finally, mercifully, trades batters.

"Don't sweat it," Diesel says as I walk off. "Baseball can be like that."

I slip into the dugout, ignore the stares and words of encouragement, and drop onto the bench beside Tommy.

"You okay?" Tommy asks.

I am, mostly. But a part of me feels . . . ashamed.

Tommy pats my leg. And just when I'm sure he'll try to comfort me, he does something else instead. "I kinda figured you got lucky yesterday," he says.

I sit there, barely able to breathe. *"What?"*

"Yesterday," Tommy repeats himself. "Noobs can't hit like—"

"Howdy, boys," we hear an all-too-familiar voice say.

Chapter 13
A Chip Off the Old Block

"Dad?"

My first thought is to **JUMP UP** and *run*. My next is to pretend I don't know the guy standing behind me.

"How's it going?" he asks.

"Aren't you supposed to be traveling for work?" I say, keeping my voice low.

"We finished early." His old leather shoes are covered with dust, and sunlight is shining on his bald head.

Clutch walks over to grab her bat and notices who I'm talking to. "This *must* be your dad!"

I pretend I didn't hear her.

"You two are practically *twins*!"

I like Dad well enough, but now all I can picture is me looking like this:

Dad winks and says, "I guess that makes Tommy the lucky one."

I just sit there, sweating on the inside.

Clutch cracks up. Then she strides to the plate and sends the first pitch into orbit.

"Wow," Dad says. "She's good."

"I know."

"She thinks we look alike," he says.

"We *don't*—trust me."

"Who's winning?"

"No one, dude! It's practice." I glance around to see if anyone is noticing us. "Where did you get that *shirt*?"

"It's hilarious, right?"

"Um . . . no."

"Don't you get it?" he asks, looking surprised that I don't. "The number is the loopback address referring to localhost. And it—"

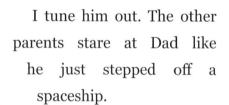

I tune him out. The other parents stare at Dad like he just stepped off a spaceship.

"—but all zeros, in terms of a route entry, usually point to the default gateway—"

"Maybe you should find some shade." I point to a spot. "There's some."

"I'm fine, actually. Maybe I'll—"

"Look," I say, raising my voice a bit, "coaches don't like parents bugging players. Here, why don't you—"

Coach Payne seems to come out of nowhere, saying, "You must be Pel's dad!"

"Tommy's, actually," Dad says.

"I'm Coach Payne."

"Douglas," Dad says.

I almost faint. The way you introduce yourself on a ball field is by calling out your last name, not your first, and maybe **SPITTING IN THE DIRT**.

Coach Payne adjusts his sunglasses and goes quiet. He doesn't want to talk to *my* parent—he wants to talk to Pel's.

"I should"—he nods toward the field—"get back."

"Sure."

Coach Payne turns and walks off—thank goodness, since this means Dad can't say something else to embarrass me.

"He seems nice," Dad says.

Coach Payne is a lot of things, but I'm not sure *nice* is one of them. "Why don't you go find that seat?"

Dad winks again, points at me, and makes a clicking sound with his mouth, all at the same time. It's the trifecta of **GEEKY DAD BEHAVIOR.** He takes a seat in the bleachers.

"What a *dork*." I turn in my seat and notice Pel eyeing me like I've done something wrong.

"He's your dad, you know," Pel says.

"You mean he's not some guy selling hot dogs?"

"Are you seriously—"

The bench starts to shake, and for a moment, I'm sure it's an earthquake. But five or six players are pounding the bench, chanting, "Turd **TANK!** Turd **TANK!**"

I've been playing rec ball enough to know what this means.

Someone has to go to the bathroom.

Chapter 14
The Turd Tank

"Turd **TANK!** Turd **TANK!**"

More players get in on the act. Alfredo has to pee—it's obvious by how he's squirming around.

"Turd **TANK!** Turd **TANK!**"

"Not happening!" Alfredo says. "I can hold it!"

The Turd Tank lies in wait. The paint on its dented exterior is fading, and the screen along the top of the door is punched out.

Alfredo gets up with his legs pressed together. He stares at the Turd Tank and says, "If I'm not out of that thing in twenty seconds, send in the cavalry." He leaps off the bench and runs across the field like a soldier charging into battle.

Pits grabs a stopwatch hanging from the fence and holds a finger over the button. Everyone knows what he intends to do. Coach Payne, Alfredo's dad, is cracking up, and Coach Decker is taking pictures of our reactions with her phone.

"Turd **TANK!** Turd **TANK!**"

Tommy gets in on the fun, chanting as loud as he can. I don't, not really, because I'm still upset by how Tommy treated his dad.

Alfredo stops in front of the old Turdle and puts on his batting glove so he won't have to touch anything. Then he pulls the neck of his shirt over his nose and throws open the door. As he enters the darkness, Pits starts the stopwatch.

Everyone starts laughing, even the parents in the stands. You don't have to be a kid or a baseball player to know the history of the Turd Tank. You just have to be from Wurtmore.

"Six seconds..." Pits calls out, **"seven...eight..."**

Clutch is clapping her hands, and Diesel is laughing so hard that her eyes are wet with tears. I'm still annoyed about Tommy.

"Ten...eleven..."

The door to the Turd Tank bangs open and Alfredo stumbles out. He runs across the field, his arms flailing.

"TIME!" Coach Payne calls out.

"Eleven seconds!" Pits says.

Everyone except me starts clapping.

Alfredo steps into the dugout, then strips off his batting glove and drops it into the trash. "That was the longest eleven seconds of my *life!*" He reaches into his backpack, pulls out a bottle of hand sanitizer, and SQUIRTS some onto his hands.

After a few minutes, the players calm down and get back to work. When batting practice ends, we run drills until we're ready to throw up, then Coach Payne tells us to meet him at the plate. Instead of a motivational speech, he tells us what we did wrong again.

Another bag of sunflower seeds gets passed around, and Diesel starts spraying shells all over the infield. Tommy's right—she's pretty amazing at everything.

"I coach my daughter's T-ball team," Coach Payne says. "We have practice after this. If anyone wants to hang around, I could use some help!"

Tommy's eyes light up. It's the perfect chance for him to get in good with the coach.

"That's all I got!" Coach Payne says, and people start gathering up their stuff. "Don't forget to have your parents check their email tonight!"

"I'm gonna stick around," Tommy says to me.

"And kiss up to the coach?" I say.

Tommy drops his jaw, pretending to be insulted.

I head for my bike and say, "Whatever. I got better things to do."

"**PEL!**" Diesel says, running up to me. "You *have* to see this T-ball team—the little kids are *adorable*! And I want to show you what was wrong with your swing today."

Tommy seems to get nervous. *He's* supposed to get in good with the Bulldogs—not me.

"Well?" Diesel says.

I think of how Tommy treated his father and realize what's really bothering me. He sometimes treats me the same way.

"Sure," I say, grinning at Tommy. "I'd love to help."

Chapter 15
The Rainbow Butterflies

Coach Payne's T-ball team is called the Rainbow Butterflies. The kids picked the name, so it's their own fault they have to spend all summer with this on their shirts:

Apparently, the runner-up for a name was the Laser Dragons, and I think that would have made for a much cooler logo.

Kindergartners are scattered across the field, and Coach Payne is at the plate, tapping soft grounders to them. Diesel, Alfredo, Goetz, Pel, and I are spread out among the kids. Our job is to make sure they're facing the right way and not picking their noses. Goetz is helping Coach Payne by fetching wild throws as they come into home. Parents are sitting on the bleachers and in lawn chairs. Most are more interested in their phones than in what's happening on the field. It's not like this is a Bulldogs game or something.

"Quit playing in the dirt!" Coach Payne yells at the second baseman, who isn't in the best position to field a ball.

"Thompson! Wake that kid up!"

"I'm on it!"

I trot up to the second baseman. "What are you doing?"

"I'm **BOOORRREEEDDD**."

"Bored?"

"I don't *like* T-ball!"

The ball thumps off Coach Payne's bat, and a slow grounder rolls past the shortstop, who's busy waving to his friend. Alfredo has to fetch the ball.

"T-ball is ***BOORRRIIINNNGGG***!"

Coach Payne points his bat at me. "Just pick him up, Thompson!"

I lift up the kid by his armpits. "C'mon— this is *fun*!"

The kid slumps his shoulders and stares at the sky, his jaw hanging open. I've never seen someone look so bored. It's impressive, actually. I bet that look buys him a lot of screen time at home.

Coach Payne points his bat at his daughter, who is twirling on first base like a ballerina. "Thompson—do something with Kessie!"

I run over to her and say, "What are you *doing*?"

Kessie stops twirling. She stands with her heels together and her toes out to the sides. She slowly squats and then stands straight again. "Plié."

"Huh?"

"I'm a dancer," Kessie says.

"Not now, you're not." I turn her to face home plate. "Right now, you're a **T-ball player**!" I try to make it sound exciting.

Kessie stands on her toes and raises her arms over her head, demonstrating another ballet move. "Relevé."

"Whatever. Just don't get pummeled by the ball, okay?" Kessie is less interested in baseball than her brother, Alfredo.

I glance over at Diesel and Pel, who have been talking all practice, standing too close to each other. When Pel says something, Diesel shifts her hips and touches his arm with her fingers. It feels like they're **FLIRTING**! But that can't be right because Pel's not interested in girls. He's interested in VIDEO GAMES.

Coach Payne swings the bat, and the ball rolls to a stop near the third baseman. He picks it up, inspects the stitching, and throws it into foul territory. Alfredo has to retrieve it.

A boy walks up and taps my leg. "What's that *smell*?"

I look around, wondering if any of the kids are young enough to be in **DIAPERS**. Then I realize the wind is blowing from the direction of center field.

"It's that," I say, pointing to the Turd Tank. "Just avoid it."

"But what if I have to go potty?" the boy says.

"I don't know. Find a bush, maybe."

Another ball gets past Pel and Diesel, who still aren't paying attention to anything but each other and **MOST DEFINITELY FLIRTING**! If they get smoochy, I'm throwing a ball at them.

Coach Payne whacks around a few more balls that Alfredo and I have to chase after.

"Mister?" a small voice says.

I look down at a boy standing beside me. "Yeah?"

"Why do you keep touching your cookies?"

"My *what*?"

"Your *cookies*." He points below my waist to show what he's talking about.

"I'm not touching my—" I realize I must be adjusting my athletic cup, which hasn't stopped bothering me. "It's a cup," I say, hoping this is enough explanation.

The boy twists his face. "You have a cup for your cookies?"

I walk off before the conversation can get me in trouble.

Coach Payne yells for everyone to bring it in. He slides a boy over to home plate like a chess piece and says, "Form a line behind this guy!" Then he points to me, Pel, Diesel, Alfredo, and Goetz. "You can take a break!"

We make our way to the dugout, and Pel practically knocks me over to get the seat next to Diesel. He takes off his ball cap and uses his shirt to wipe his sweaty brow.

"That's a *serious* mullet," Alfredo says.

"It's not a mullet," Pel says.

"Oh, yes, it is," Alfredo says. **"Business in the front, party in the back."**

Alfredo always knows the coolest things to say. I can totally see him being an Internet star someday.

Mullet Sightings! ⋮
Alfredo-Tube
509,102 views – 2 days ago

"I like your hair," Diesel says. "It's retro."

Pel looks away, blushing like a little kid. It's like he's falling in love or something, and I'm about two seconds away from throwing up.

Goetz reaches into his backpack and pulls out a bag of sunflower seeds. He takes some and passes them around. After a minute, Pel spits a shell into an empty bubble gum bucket being used as a garbage can. It's hard to believe he's showing off with something *I* taught him.

Not to be outdone, I crack a shell between my teeth and spit both pieces into the bucket.

Pel stops fawning over Diesel long enough to give me a dirty look. Then he loads a few more seeds into his mouth and lands their shells in the bucket.

"*C'mon*, Pel!" Alfredo says. "You can't beat **Timmy** at everything."

I can't take it anymore, especially the part about Alfredo getting my name wrong. I score three shells and take the lead.

Pel glares at me.

I glare back.

And just like that, **it's on.**

Chapter 16
What the Helianthus?

Tommy targets the bucket, spits, and misses. Two seconds later, I score again. Goetz grabs his phone and starts recording a video, which probably puts the pressure on Tommy. Tommy scores two, back-to-back, and I hit three in a row.

"Whoa! Check out *Mullet Man!*" Alfredo says. "Going to *work!*"

It's another nickname for me. I guess I'm winning that contest too.

"Way to go, kid!" Coach Payne hollers.

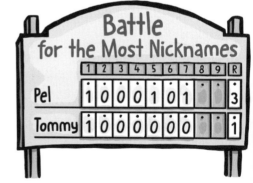

Battle for the Most Nicknames

	1	2	3	4	5	6	7	8	9	R
Pel	1	0	0	0	1	0	1			3
Tommy	1	0	0	0	0	0	0			1

At first, I think he's talking to me. But then I realize someone made it to first base.

I spit another shell that lands in the bucket. I've already lost track of the score, but this could be a situation where the last point wins.

Tommy nails another shot. And another. It's one area in life where he's really improving.

On the field, some kid runs to the pitcher's mound instead of first, and a girl **JUMPS** on second like it's a trampoline. On the bench, the battle continues—

—and continues—

—and continues.

When Tommy loads more seeds into his mouth, something wrong happens, and he sprays the seeds everywhere.

"Dude—you all right?" Alfredo asks.

Tommy nods and tries to play it cool, but it seems like he can hardly breathe. A seed must be stuck in his throat.

"Tommy?" I say.

He jumps to his feet, as if that's going to help, and staggers around. I turn to the field, hoping Coach Payne noticed what's happening. But he's busy trying to get the kid at second base to put his pants back on.

"*Was stimmt nicht mit ihm?*" Goetz says, as if any of us speaks German.

Tommy continues fighting for air. Wurtmore Park suddenly seems like the dumbest place in the world to die.

"*Dad!*" Alfredo says. "Someone's choking!"

Someone. And Tommy probably thought being called "Timmy" was bad.

Coach Payne looks our way and charges across the field. A bunch of Rainbow Butterflies chase after him, probably thinking it's a game. Coach Payne **LEAPS** into the dugout and stands in front of Tommy, his eyes full of fear.

"He swallowed a seed!" I say.

"*What?*" Coach Payne asks.

"A *seed*!"

The Rainbow Butterflies crowd the dugout.

Parents jump out of their seats and gather around the team. "Who knows the Heimlich?" a man with a shaggy beard asks.

When no one answers, I hold my phone up to my face and say into the mic, "How do you do the Heimlich maneuver?"

A woman's voice comes through the speaker: "Make a fist, place it above the navel, and—"

WWHHAAAPPP!!

Goetz slaps Tommy's back so hard that the seed shoots from his mouth. For a second, I see it floating in the air, wet with spit. Then it sticks to the **WORST PLACE** I can imagine.

Tommy leans forward, still fighting to catch his breath. A boy offers his water bottle. Tommy grabs it and takes a few swigs.

"You okay?" Coach Payne asks.

Tommy sips more water, coughs a few times, and finally catches his breath. Then he turns to me, saying, **"THIS IS *YOUR* FAULT!"**

"Mine?"

"You have to make a contest out of **everything**!"

I blink a few times. "What are—"

"Are those snacks?" a boy calls out to a woman with a large box in her hands.

The woman nods. "Brownies."

The Rainbow Butterflies jump around, asking if they can have some.

"Is it okay to share?" the woman asks Coach Payne, holding up the box.

"Fine with me." Coach Payne flicks the seed off his glasses and walks out of the dugout. "I've had enough ball for today."

The woman opens the box of brownies, and Goetz is the first in line.

I point to Tommy and say, "*You're* the one who makes a contest out of everything."

"I do *not*!" Tommy snaps back.

I step out of the dugout to help Diesel pick up the batting gear—and to get away from Tommy.

Tommy takes a seat on the bench and waits. Once it's obvious I'm in no hurry, he grabs his stuff and heads for his bike. I watch him ride off, happy that his trip home is going to be lonely.

Chapter 17
Cutting the Mustard

"Ma! Your password is 'rescueme,' one word, right?"

"Did you capitalize the *R*?"

I try the password with the capital letter, and it works this time. A new email from Coach Payne is at the top of the inbox. I look away, worried it could read like this:

Dear Parent,

This email is to inform you that your son, **THOMAS THOMPSON**, did not make the second round of cuts. I wish I had better news, but unfortunately **THOMAS THOMPSON** is not a very good player and misses a lot of pop-ups. Please tell **THOMAS THOMPSON** we look forward to seeing him in the stands.

Sincerely,

Coach Payne

"Ma, *come here!*"

"I'm doing the dishes."

"You're *always* doing the dishes!"

"That's because you're always eating!"

"I need some—"

The faucet shuts off, and Ma utters a few words that I would get in trouble for using. She stomps into the room and stands with her arms crossed. ***"What?"***

I back away from the desk and say, "Can you read Coach Payne's email?"

Ma moves across the room and says, "You're something else, kid." She drops into the chair, clicks the mouse a couple times, and starts reading: "'Dear Parent, Thomas Thompson is invited to participate in day three of the four-day tryouts for the Bulldogs. Please make sure Thomas Thompson—'"

I lean across Ma to finish reading. "'—is at Wurtmore Park tomorrow at 1:00. I look forward to seeing Thomas Thompson.'"

"LOOKS LIKE YOU MADE IT," Ma says.

I barely believe it. I almost expect Ma to say ***Oops!*** and click on a different email—the *right* email, which says I'm the **biggest** loser in Wurtmore.

Ma stands up and kisses my cheek. "Good job, little man." She pats my back and heads into the kitchen.

I read the email again and again. It's the best news I've had since . . . well, yesterday. I pull out my phone to text Pel before remembering what happened today. I tell myself to be the better person and tap my fingers across the screen.

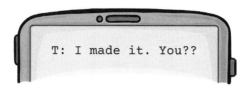

I stare at the phone and wait for a response.

He's probably playing video games, I think to myself.

I wait some more.

And some more.

His reply never comes.

Chapter 18
Batting Practice

I stare at my phone and read Tommy's text again.

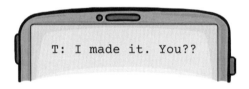

T: I made it. You??

I tap the message to open a dialogue box but can't bring myself to reply. Tommy was a jerk today.

The cursor blinks in the empty box, beckoning me to tap my fingertips across the keys. I inch my finger closer to the screen, but before I can touch it, my phone rings. It's an unknown number.

"Hello?" I say, answering the call.

"Pel?" comes a familiar voice. It takes me a moment to place it.

I sit up in my chair, feeling nervous. **"Diesel?"**

"I got your number from Coach Payne," Diesel says. "Did you make the cut?"

"I did."

"I knew you would," she says with a bit of excitement in her voice. "Listen—what are you doing right now?"

"Nothing." It's actually true. Up until the moment Tommy texted, I was sitting in my chair, staring across the room.

"Can you switch to a video call?" she asks. "I want to show you what was wrong with your swing today. I didn't get a chance at T-ball practice."

I pause to process everything. Diesel, maybe the most popular member of the Bulldogs, *and* Tommy's stupid Super Sports Society, just called me. And she wants to help *me* make the team.

"Pel?" she says. "You still there?"

"Yeah."

"You'll need a bat. And some room to swing."

I nod, forgetting she can't see me yet. "Okay, give me a second." I mute the call and hurry out of my room, suddenly anxious about everything. I bump into the hallway wall and stumble on the stairs.

"You all right?" Mom says, sitting at the kitchen table.

I nod. "I'm taking a video call with someone from the Bulldogs."

"That's my Pel," she says. "What's his name?"

"Diesel," I answer. "She's a girl."

The corners of Mom's mouth curl upward. Thankfully, she doesn't press.

In the garage, I rummage through the storage until I find a plastic bat that's easily a foot shorter than it needs to be.

When I switch the call to video, Diesel appears on the screen. She's standing in her yard, holding a bat, and her phone is stationed on something about ten feet away. But she can still see me, because she asks, **"IS THAT YOUR ONLY BAT?"**

I feel my cheeks flush red-hot with embarrassment. "Sorry."

"It'll work. I want to focus on your foundation anyway."

I nod, pretending to know what she means. Then I set my phone down on a shelf and stand in the middle of the open space.

"First your grip," she says. "Line up your door-knocking knuckles on the bat." She holds her hands closer to her phone to show what she means. "Keep the bat out on your fingertips, not on your palm. Your bottom hand should be tighter than the top—this keeps your back arm free."

I follow her instructions the best I can, decoding some of the BASEBALL SPEAK. Then I hold my hands to the screen to show her my grip.

"Good," she says. "And you can personalize the grip a bit—the bat should feel comfortable in your hands."

She goes on to explain a few things about a good batter's stance. Your feet should be even in the box and a bit wider than your shoulders. You should flex your knees and angle your spine. You should stay relaxed but ready at the same time. Loose muscles are fast.

"Nice," she says, studying my stance. "Now, let's focus on your swing."

She tells me to load my weight against my back side and stride forward, dancing with the pitcher. Your power comes from your legs, and your core controls your body.

"Try it," she says. **"Let me see a full swing."**

I grip the toy bat and arrange my body the way she explained. Then I load my weight and stride forward, pivoting at the waist. My arms loop around, and at the end of my swing, the smooth plastic bat slips out of my hands and flies out into the driveway. Diesel and I burst out laughing.

"I think we need to work on your grip," she says.

We keep laughing until it hurts. Before I can retrieve my bat, another call comes into my phone, and I lean forward to see who it is.

"Is someone calling you?" Diesel asks. "I can hear a soft buzzing on my end. Answer it."

"That's okay." I swipe a finger across the screen to dismiss the call. "It's **NOBODY**."

It feels partly true, at least at the moment.

Tommy was calling.

And I'd much rather spend time with Diesel.

Chapter 19
Tommy Takes Two

On Friday afternoon, I pull up to the field by myself and frown when I find Pel's bike near the dugout. It's unbelievable that he'd ride to tryouts without me because of a little spat, but I guess he did.

I drop my bike and helmet, grab my glove from my backpack, and head onto the diamond, where the players are warming up. There are four new Bulldogs in addition to the ones who've already been helping out.

"We're scrimmaging today," says Coach Decker, who stands beside me, holding a clipboard.

"How many people got cut?" I ask.

"We're down to ten candidates. You're one of 'em, so **CONGRATS**."

A part of me can hardly believe I made it this far. If I survive cuts today, I'll be playing in the Bulldog Brawl tomorrow. And if I make that cut, I'll have a spot on the team. I know I act all tough, but this has been a dream **F O R E V E R**. I really hope nothing messes it up.

Pel is playing catch with Diesel, so I do some stretches to get loose. Before long, Coach Decker divides us into teams, and Pel and I end up together. We're first to bat. I grab a seat next to him on the bench.

"What happened?" I ask.

Pel looks like he has no clue what I'm talking about.

"Last night. You never texted me back."

"I was busy." He takes a batting glove out of his back pocket and slips it on. It's about two sizes too big.

"Where'd you get that?"

"Someone gave it to me," he says.

"Who?"

I can tell he doesn't want to answer.

"It was Goetz, wasn't it?" Only one kid's hands are that big.

Pel shrugs to show it's no big deal. "He had an extra one he never uses."

I shake my head. I'm supposed to be getting in good with the Bulldogs—not Pel!

Diesel finishes strapping on her catcher's gear and steps onto the field. The defense takes their positions, and Javon Anderson, a seventh grader who plays for the Bulldogs, delivers the first pitch. It's a swing and miss for Noah Cardoso, our first batter.

"Can you do something for me?" I ask.

"If it's call out your nickname, no."

I draw my head back. "Why can't—"

"Hey!" Coach Decker shouts. "Who's on deck?"

Pits grabs a bat and hurries into the on-deck circle. When Cardoso strikes out on the next pitch, Pits struts up to the plate with the confidence of a travel player. He leans back into his stance, looking ready to rip the cover off the ball.

"Can I ask you something?" I lean in close to Pel so no one else can hear me. "You have a *thing* for Diesel, don't you?"

"A *thing*?"

"A crush."

He plays it off by laughing.

HA, HA, HA!

I lean in closer and touch his shoulder. "I saw her bump you with her hip."

"When?"

"Yesterday," I say, "at T-ball practice."

"I don't—"

"That's *way* flirty, bro."

Pel rolls his eyes. "Whatever, dude."

"Thompson!" Coach Decker calls out. "Grab a bat, would ya?"

I slip on a helmet and try to get my head back into baseball. "I need a hit—big-time."

"Keep your eye on the ball," Pel says, "and swing through the pitch."

"Yeah, thanks. I learned that about two hundred years ago." I tap Pel's shoulder and add, "Remember . . . *Tommy Twice*."

"It's all about you—I haven't forgotten."

I'm not sure what he means, but it seems like a way of calling me a jerk. "You know," I say, "you've been so moody since this Diesel thing."

"*Diesel thing*? Are you—"

I walk off before Pel can lie about being madly in love.

"Go get 'em, son!" says a familiar voice. Dad just got here and is walking up to the field. I wave. I'm happy he's here, but not happy enough to do a repeat of yesterday. Thankfully, he gets the picture, and I watch him settle in with the other parents.

After the kid batting behind Pits gets robbed of a double, it's my turn at the plate. I walk up, adjust my cup because it's pinching and pulling, and take a spot in the batter's box.

"Uh-oh," Diesel says. "It's **LORD VADER**."

I'm pretty sure I'll be hearing *Star Wars* jokes for the rest of my life.

Anderson, the pitcher, has narrow eyes and a spatter of pimples on his chin. His shirt reads **LIFE'S A PITCH.** He'd never get away with something like that in rec league.

The first ball blows right past me and **WHAPS** in Diesel's glove.

"ALL RIGHT, NOW!" Coach Payne hollers from his position as the first base coach. "BE A HITTER!"

I step out of the box, tap my cleats with my bat, and then step back in. Anderson settles into his stance. When the pitch comes, I swing late, and dust rises like smoke out of Diesel's mitt.

"QUICK HANDS!" Coach Payne says. "C'MON, NOW!"

I step back and take a few practice swings. Then I move back to the plate and dig in like a tick.

"Easy swing," Diesel advises me. "Let the bat do the work."

Anderson goes through his motions, his limbs bending and extending like the legs of a praying mantis. I swing at the next pitch and shoot a ground ball gapper between third and short. I flip the bat and charge down the first baseline, hoping everyone is noticing.

The infielders scramble into position. When Coach Payne yells, **"GO TWO! GO TWO!"** I can't help but think of Roy Davis and his record-setting time in the Turd Tank.

I round first base, springing off the inside corner.

The **SUN BEATS DOWN**...

...my *CLEATS SHRED THE EARTH*...

...and I **SWALLOW A BUG THE SIZE OF A PEA**.

The second baseman holds out his glove, waiting for a throw from the outfield.

"YOU'RE DOWN! YOU'RE DOWN!" Coach Payne yells.

Because normal slides are for wimps, I go in like this—

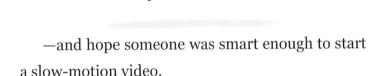

—and hope someone was smart enough to start a slow-motion video.

I slam down, and a wave of dirt pours over me. Blinded by dust, I reach for second base, and when I feel the warm leather, I grab it. The incoming ball hits my head, and my helmet pops off. Both roll into right-center.

I jump up, thinking of **HOW INCREDIBLY EPIC** it would be to stretch a double into a triple. But after I take a few strides, the world seems to topple. I stumble out of the baseline and collapse near Clutch, the shortstop. The ball must have hit me harder than I thought.

"Hey, you okay?" Clutch says, leaning over me. A titanium chain dangles from her neck, and her nostrils are two dark ovals.

"Am I safe?" I ask.

The answer comes as someone strolls up and tags my leg with the ball.

I lie there, wishing the throw had taken off my head along with the helmet. The earth trembles, and Coach Payne appears next to Clutch; they're both looking down at me.

"Thompson!" Coach Payne says, sounding both worried and annoyed. "You okay?"

"Yes?" I meant to put a period in place of the question mark.

Dad runs up and leans over, trying to catch his breath. He shouldn't be running—he gets winded when checking the mail.

"Tommy?" Dad says.

Coach Payne again pulls out his *Wurtmore Parks Youth Sport Manual* and flips to a page—the one with the concussion protocol, no doubt.

"Choose three of the following words," he reads. "*Dog, blue, car, mailbox, tree, hamster.* You got 'em?"

"Yeah."

"Which ones did you pick?" he asks.

"TREE, **HAMSTER**, *CAR*"

"Okay, now remember them." He turns to a new page and starts reading again. "What do you recall just prior to the impact?"

"Getting hit in the head."

"How did you get to the park?" he asks.

"My bike."

"Okay, now tell me the words you picked from the list."

"Huh?"

"The list," he says. "What three words did you choose?"

I have to think about it. "*Hamster . . . tree . . .* and *cat.*"

Coach Payne looks over at Dad. "Was *cat* an option?"

Dad shrugs. "I wasn't paying attention."

"Me either." Coach Payne tosses the manual aside and lifts me up by my armpits. "Let's do this the old-school way."

Coach Payne and Dad help me off the field. A few people start clapping, which only makes it more embarrassing. Goetz staggers around, imitating me. And worse, Pel is laughing with him.

I pull away from Coach Payne and Dad and walk past everyone on the bench, nearly tripping over a few feet. Then I drop into a seat beside Pel, who immediately stops laughing.

"Something funny?" I ask.

"Sorry, man," he says. "But you should have seen yourself!"

"Dude, I could have been—"

"Why didn't you settle for the double?" he interrupts.

"Because I had a chance to make third on the overthrow!"

"Who cares?" he says. "You were already in scoring position."

"What do you know about *baseball*? You're just SOME GUY WHO PLAYS VIDEO GAMES!"

Pel's face drops. "*Excuse* me?"

"You shouldn't even be out here!"

"Pel!" Coach Decker shouts. "You're up!"

Pel squints at me. Then he grabs a bat and points it at me as he marches onto the field. "You asked for this, Tommy Twice."

Chapter 20
The Moon Shot

I step into the box, scowling. I smack my bat against the plate—**WHUMP!**—and dig in my back foot.

"Wow," Diesel says. "Someone came to play."

I lift my bat and focus on the pitcher, Anderson. Tommy's latest insult—that I'm just some guy who plays video games—echoes in my head. When the pitch comes, I *SMACK* the ball over the left fielder's head and take off running.

I round first base, second base, and then third. Before the throw comes in, my cleats touch down on home plate. Some of the Bulldogs clap, but most of the bench—the kids fighting for a spot on the team—stay quiet.

"NICE SHOT," Diesel says. As I circle back for the bat, she fist-bumps me.

"Pel—hold up for a sec!" Coach Payne says. He looks over at the bench and yells, "Thompson!"

"Yeah?" Tommy says.

"Bring out a bucket!"

Tommy grabs a bucket of balls, takes it to the mound, and heads back to the bench. I can tell by his face that he's annoyed Coach is turning him into a bucket boy.

"Hit a few more!" Coach Payne tells me. Then he nods at Coach Decker, clearly communicating something.

Diesel and I return to our spots.

"Stay loose," Diesel says. "Just swing the bat—don't try to rip the cover off the ball."

I lift my bat over my shoulder and drive the next pitch over Clutch's head.

"NICE!" Coach Payne says. **"There's the swing we saw the first day!"** He looks at Coach Decker, and this time she nods at him.

Anderson reaches his hand into the bucket. When he delivers the next pitch, I send it into shallow right.

"Looking good!" Coach Decker says.

I put the next ball into deep left and the two after that into center field.

"Throw him your heat!" Coach Payne tells Anderson.

It's baseball jargon that I haven't learned yet. I must appear confused because Diesel says, "Here comes a fastball."

The pitch arrives as advertised, and I smash it down the third baseline with a **CRACK** of the bat. Everyone on the bench looks stunned—especially Tommy.

I step out of the box and tap my cleats with my bat, feeling like I'm prepping for the next round of battle.

"Drop one off the table!" Coach Decker tells Anderson.

"It's a **BREAKING BALL**," Diesel says, just loud enough for me to hear.

I have no idea what a breaking ball is, but when the next pitch comes, it dips at the last second, and I have to lower my swing to make contact. The ball rolls past the mound and into the outfield.

"Way to adjust," Diesel says. She claps her hand against the palm of her mitt.

Coach Payne turns to a Bulldog I don't recognize and says, "Kid's never played before."

"You're joking, right?" the Bulldog says.

"Nope. Never picked up a bat until this week."

It's not exactly true. I used to play with the plastic bat that's kept in the garage. I might have been six years old then, but hey, it *has* happened before this week.

I connect with the **NEXT PITCH**, and the **NEXT**, and the **NEXT**. Of the eight pitches after that, I connect with six. Coach Payne seems stunned, and Coach Decker is impressed. Tommy looks terrified.

"Last one!" Anderson says while pulling a final ball out of the bucket.

I bend my knees and load my weight, thinking of everything Diesel taught me: door-knocking knuckles aligned, muscles loose, feet just wider than my shoulders. I imagine how **AWESOME** it would be to clobber one now.

Diesel's mitt opens like the mouth of a catfish, and Anderson delivers the final pitch. I stride forward, pivoting at the waist. The ball connects squarely with the bat—

WWRRAAAACCCKKK!

—and soars into center field, looking like it might have the distance to reach the woods.

"No *way*," comes a small voice from the bench. Tommy.

The ball leaves the field and **THUMPS** against the Turd Tank, scaring a squirrel out from inside it.

When the field erupts in laughter and applause, it's all I can do not to mic-drop the bat.

"That was a total **MOON SHOT!**" Diesel says, standing behind the plate.

More baseball speak, and I smile because a moon shot sounds like a good thing. I give Diesel another fist bump, fully aware that our knuckles are touching again.

"I told ya!" Coach Decker says to Coach Payne, and I can't help but wonder what she means.

I strut off the field, holding the middle of the bat. I'm not sure I've ever felt so **good**, so **alive**. I can feel the heat on my face and the air in my lungs, like I'm breathing for the first time ever.

I reach the dugout. As I stride along the bench, the Bulldogs greet me with high fives.

"All right, *enough!*" Coach Payne shouts. "Someone get that ball for Pel—**that souvenir belongs on his shelf!**"

I throw down my bat and helmet, and someone hands me a cup of water. I walk along the bench with my chest puffed out.

I pass Tommy, intentionally bump his knees, and take the seat farthest from him.

I chug the water and **CRUMPLE** the cup, confident that Tommy now knows I'm **NOT** just "some guy who plays video games."

Chapter 21
Life Isn't All Rainbows and Butterflies

"KHOOOOH PUUUHRR ... KHOOOOH PUUUHRR ..."

It's the sound of Darth Vader breathing, but I'm not making it.

"KHOOOOH PUUUHRR ..."

Goetz walks up to me, grinning from ear to ear like he did in the sporting goods store. "You *won't* know the *power* of the dark side."

"It's *don't*, you dork."

"KHOOOOH PUUUHRR ..."

Coach Payne asked us to stick around for another Rainbow Butterflies practice. Dad went home, and the parents in the bleachers changed from Bulldog tryout parents to Rainbow Butterflies parents. Goetz, Pel, Diesel, and I are helping in the field; Coach Payne is working with the batters; and Alfredo is trying to control the kids in the dugout. I'm standing near first base, and Goetz just drifted over from center to give me a hard time.

"Hey, Thompson," he says. "I got a nickname for you!"

I roll my eyes and wait to hear it.

"*Fart Vader.*" He chuckles, clearly proud of himself. "Get it?"

I stroll toward the first baseline, hoping Goetz will take the hint. He must, because he heads back to his spot, breathing like Darth Vader again.

Parents are sitting in the bleachers and on lawn chairs. A few clap when Kessie steps up to the plate.

"Hi, Dad!" Kessie says to Coach Payne, who's standing just outside the batter's box.

Coach Payne touches his daughter's shoulder and places a ball on the tee. "Here you go, Kes."

Kessie takes a swing and knocks over the tee.

"Eyes on the ball," her father says, fixing the tee.

Kessie tries again and again and finally, at long last, makes contact. The results aren't as impressive as they could be.

"RUN!" her father hollers, startling her a bit.

"Where?"

"THERE!" He points to where she needs to go, and Kessie skips down the first baseline. The entire infield descends on the ball, and it's pretty clear they'll need more coaching on some fundamentals.

A few parents cheer as Kessie jumps onto the base and strikes a ballerina pose: heels together, toes out to the sides, a bend in her knees. I know from our first practice that it's a plié. It's pretty impressive, but it's not for the baseball field.

"Stop that," I say.

"Stop what?" She bends her knees out to the sides, lowering her rear end.

"Pretty much everything you're doing." I grab Kessie's shoulders and set her up in a base-runner stance. "Here. Like this."

Across the field, Pel and Diesel are standing too close and giggling. You're not supposed to giggle in baseball. THURMAN MUNSON never giggled. *Kelsie Whitmore* never giggled. David Ortiz never giggled. Bo Jackson used to break bats over his head.

A boy named Petey steps up to the plate. After what seems like a hundred swings, he manages to tap the ball off the tee. It rolls to a stop in the same spot as Kessie's.

"*GO!*" Coach Payne shouts.

Petey takes off, and the infielders charge the ball and end up in another heap. Petey steps onto first base like a soldier claiming a hill.

"I want you to lead off the bag," I say.

"Huh?"

"Take a few steps away from the bag," I explain. "That way you can get to second base faster."

"Why would I want to leave?" Petey says. "I just got here!"

I grab his shoulders and move him off the bag.

"Hey!" Coach Payne shouts. **"NO LEADOFFS!"**

"Seriously?"

"No stealing bases and no slides! This is T-ball, Thompson—not the majors!"

I groan and pull Petey back to the bag.

More Butterflies get a chance to bat. I watch as Pel and Diesel become more cringey than ever—**giggling** and TOUCHING and standing too close.

Goetz graduates from Darth Vader impressions to other *Star Wars* characters: Chewbacca, Jabba the Hutt, Grogu, and an impressive Jar Jar Binks. Meanwhile, I'm doing everything I can to help, and Coach Payne is hardly noticing.

The last batter is a girl named Darla. She steps into the box, half buries her back foot, and lines up the ball with the barrel of the bat. She has bright red hair, her shoulders are as big as mine, and she's wearing a Metallica T-shirt instead of her uniform. Most kids don't wear band T-shirts to practice, but I can't fault her for taste.

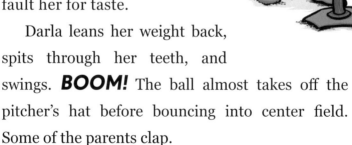

Darla leans her weight back, spits through her teeth, and swings. **BOOM!** The ball almost takes off the pitcher's hat before bouncing into center field. Some of the parents clap.

"GO! GO! GO!" Diesel says to the runners. It's nice to see her head in the game for a change.

More parents realize what's happening and erupt in applause. The left fielder runs for the ball because the center fielder isn't going to be much help.

The catcher trips on the plate and can't get up because of his clunky gear. The runner coming in from third scores.

"Oh no!" Goetz says in a C-3PO voice. "Throw it *in*! Throw it *in*!"

Another run scores as Coach Payne helps the catcher to his feet. The left fielder picks up the ball and does a pretty good job of slinging it in. The ball rolls to a stop about halfway to the plate, and the catcher waddles out to get it, the buckles of a dozen loose straps **CLANKING** against his gear.

The third run scores, leaving only Darla on base. She rounds third at what must be a hundred miles 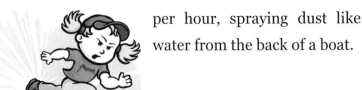 per hour, spraying dust like water from the back of a boat.

Darla's the Diesel of the Rainbow Butterflies.

The catcher picks up the ball and runs toward the plate—*CLINK! CLANK! CLINK!*—with his glove held out.

"GO, DARLA!" Diesel yells.

The catcher gets tangled in his gear and falls again just as Darla's cleats come down on the plate.

The crowd goes nuts. Diesel and Pel cheer and jump and hang on to each other.

I just stand there by myself, feeling like a jerk.

"Beep-beep-boo. Beep-doo-weep!"

Great. R2-D2 is coming.

I head off the field before Goetz can get close. I grab my bag from the dugout, unlock my bike, and ride off. It hurts when no one tries to stop me.

Halfway across the parking lot, I slam on the brakes, spitting gravel out to one side.

This isn't the way to make the team, I think. *Worse, it's cowardly.* THURMAN MUNSON *wouldn't do this. Neither would* **Kelsie Whit-more** *or* David Ortiz *or* **Bo Jackson**.

I turn around and pedal back to the field. The Rainbow Butterflies' parents are already corralling their kids, and Pel and the Bulldogs are packing up the team gear. I drop my bike and hurry over, intent on helping. But when I get close, I overhear Alfredo and Diesel inviting Pel to watch the **big game** with them later today.

I freeze in my tracks, barely believing all that's going wrong. Everyone loves Pel, and I'm just someone who isn't going to make the team.

I turn around, jump back on my bike, and race for the exit, feeling like **the world is ending.**

Chapter 22
The Dog Pound

I stand on the porch and stare at the door, too intimidated to knock. The Dog Pound is just inside Coach Payne's house, but it's not a place I ever expected to visit. Suddenly worried that I read Diesel's text wrong, I pull out my phone and gaze at the screen.

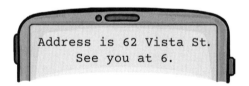

Address is 62 Vista St.
See you at 6.

I read the text a few more times, but the message doesn't change. The Bulldogs invited me to their secret hangout.

"**Okay, Pel,**" I say to myself. "**You got this.**"

I raise my hand and rap my knuckles on the door. Heavy footsteps sound inside, and then the door swings open, revealing Coach Payne. Framed by the entrance, he looks bigger than ever, and somehow it isn't so surprising that he's wearing his sunglasses inside.

"It's my boy Pel!" Coach Payne says, reaching out for a fist bump.

I tap my tiny knuckles against his. "Hi, Coach."

"Come on in!" he says, stepping out of the way. He points to the basement stairs and adds, "Everyone's in the Pound."

I smile to say thanks and head in that direction, more nervous than ever. I'm **PEL**, the **quiet kid** in the back of the room, THE GAMER. I'm not cool or popular, and I certainly don't hang out with members of the Super Sports Society at their Super Sports Dog Pound or whatever.

I slowly take the steps and nearly gasp as the Dog Pound appears before me.

"**PEL!**" Diesel shouts, turning on the couch to get a better look at me.

I force a smile, still feeling weird about everything.

Alfredo walks over and claps my back so hard that I nearly fall forward. **"Welcome to the Pound, Moon Shot!"**

Another nickname. If Tommy were here, he'd be more jealous than ever.

Something about the idea makes me feel guilty. Tommy *should* be here, not me. He's the one who's dreamed about being a Bulldog. The Dog Pound is more magical to him than a theme park.

"You want some pizza?" Alfredo says and points to a box on the table.

"No, thanks," I say. Uh-oh. Was I too polite? When I'm with the Bulldogs, they're usually spitting in the dirt and trying to look tough.

"Chips?" Alfredo asks.

I shake my head.

"Okay then," Alfredo says. He gestures to the room with a sweep of his arm. "*Mi casa es tu casa*." It means "My house is your house." And it reminds me that Alfredo was in my fourth-grade Spanish class.

Diesel scoots over on the couch, making room for me. "Here—have a seat."

I almost don't want to. Diesel's a girl, after all, and sitting so close to her could be uncomfortable for a bunch of reasons. But I also **REALLY, REALLY** want to.

"I don't bite," she adds.

I smile and hope the heat in my cheeks isn't showing. Then I scuttle forward and take a seat that feels dangerously close to her.

"What do you think of the place?" she asks.

I gaze around the room: the sports posters and pennants, the workout equipment, the big-screen TV with the baseball game playing. It's exactly the kind of place where I would have imagined the Bulldogs hang out—**the perfect place for Tommy**. The thought makes me feel guilty again.

"It's really cool," I manage to say.

Diesel smiles and winks at me.

"Who are you rooting for?" Pits asks, nodding to the TV. His fingers are laced behind his head, and through his muscle shirt, his hairy armpits are on full display.

"Who's playing?" I ask.

Pits eyes me like he can't believe I asked the question.

"The Yankees and the Red Sox," Diesel says, rescuing me. "It's the second inning."

Pits talks about the game—the players and what's been happening. With all the baseball slang, I hardly understand what he's saying. A ribbie sounds like an inflatable raft, and a worm burner sounds horrifying.

Pits, Diesel, and I ease into a conversation about other things: summer vacation, a rock band coming to town, and what life at Wurtmore Middle School is going to be like. At some point, Alfredo takes a seat in the chair beside Pits and starts weaving jokes into everything being said. He's the funniest person I've ever met and far less intense than his dad. After some time, I grab a slice of pizza and a handful of chips.

"WHO'S NEXT?" Goetz asks during the fifth inning of the game. He's standing by the foosball table, hoping for a new challenger, and motions to me. "Mullet Man, you play foosball the way you hit?"

I wave off the invitation. I'm not even sure what foosball is.

"C'mon, Pel!" Diesel says, rising to her feet. "I'll be your partner."

I spring off the couch quicker than I meant to. There's no way I'll pass on a chance to be Diesel's partner at anything.

Diesel and I share one side of the foosball table, each of us operating two rods that control the players. The object of the game is simple: score as many goals as you can, and Goetz is **REALLY GOOD** at it. He wins every time but doesn't brag about it like Tommy would.

After a few games, Diesel and I return to our former spots on the couch. Goetz joins us, but his muscles crowd the space, which prompts Diesel and I to sit closer than ever.

Talking to the Bulldogs gets easier and easier, and a part of me realizes I'm fitting in. In the baseball game on TV, the fifth inning becomes the sixth, and the Yankees take the lead. I'm surprised the commercials aren't my favorite part to watch.

"Anyone want a soda?" Alfredo asks.

A few of us accept the offer, and Alfredo rises from his chair. He takes a few steps and stops, his gaze locked on something behind me. He says something that sounds like "Thompson," but it can't be Thompson, because that would mean Tommy is here.

I wonder if I heard him right. After deciding I didn't, I turn my head to follow Alfredo's stare and barely believe what I see.

Tommy is standing at the base of the stairs.

Chapter 23
2 Legit 2 Quit

"Tommy?" Pel says. He looks more surprised than Alfredo to see me. "What are you doing?"

I try to answer, but the words won't form. My eyes scan the pennants, the posters, the baseball game on the TV. The Dog Pound is all around me.

"Tommy?" Pel tries again.

I snap out of my wonder and gaze at Pel. He seems out of focus compared to the rest of the room.

"What are you—" Pel starts.

"I was riding by and saw your bike." It's a lie, of course, the one I've been rehearsing. Pel's mom told me Pel went to Alfredo's house when I saw her walking home.

I pull the Wurtmore Games gift card out of my pocket and show it to him. "I meant to give you this at practice today."

"Oh." Pel flicks his gaze around the room, as if to see how the Bulldogs are reacting. "Okay."

I stride across the basement and **bump** into a steel arm of the foosball table, pretending it didn't hurt. At the couch, I hold out the gift card.

"Thanks," Pel says and takes the card.

"No problem, bro." I stand there, smiling and waiting for an invite to stick around.

It doesn't happen . . .

Then it still doesn't happen . . .

Then it still doesn't happen some more . . .

Finally, Alfredo says, "You wanna watch the game with us?"

"Sure!" I spit out before Alfredo can change his mind. The only open seat is a rocking chair. It's kind of small, but I manage to fit.

"Who's winning?" I ask, pretending that everything is fine and normal and not awkward at all.

"The Yanks," Pel says. "They're up two."

I smile, surprised that Pel knows the nickname of the Yankees, and gaze around the room. The foosball table, the gym equipment, the salty snacks, the sugary drinks. The Dog Pound is everything I imagined it would be—a super sports hangout for a Super Sports Society! I could spend the rest of my life here.

"I never thought I'd see Fart Vader in the Pound," Goetz says, looking at me. **"KHOOOOH PUUUHRR . . . POOOOOOFT."**

It's funny, but it isn't something I should laugh at. Pits does, and Pel giggles a bit, which is a little annoying.

"Is there pizza?" I ask, noticing a half-eaten piece on a plate.

Alfredo raises one eyebrow and stares at me like he doesn't want to answer. But maybe that's just in my head. I relax a bit when he says, "Pepperoni. You want some?"

"Sure, thanks!"

Alfredo lifts his eyebrow a little higher, gets up, and walks across the room. He quickly returns and drops a paper plate with a cold pizza slice in my lap. The pizza almost falls to the floor.

The sixth inning of the game ends. When the game cuts to a commercial featuring a bus, Alfredo says, **"OH, I GOTTA SHOW YOU GUYS SOMETHING!"** He jumps up, pulls out his phone, and walks over to Diesel.

"A bus?" Diesel says, squinting at the screen.

"My dad's thinking about buying it for the team!"

"Seriously?" she says. "That's *awesome!*"

The phone gets passed around the room and eventually makes it to me. The bus is one of the **coolest things** I've ever seen!

I can totally see it rolling down the street with the Bulldogs sitting two in a row, snacking on chips and dips, and holding their heads out the windows because someone keeps farting.

"Has your dad picked any tourneys yet?" Diesel asks.

"Yeah, one in Myrtle Beach," Alfredo says. "And we'll be going to Florida again."

"Jacksonville?" Pits says. "Sweet."

The Bulldogs share a few stories about their traveling adventures. In Iowa, Clutch's mother swerved off the highway to miss a deer and barreled through a cornfield. In Missouri, Pits got stuck in a hotel elevator for three hours. In Florida, Tower fell asleep at the hotel pool and missed the first game of a doubleheader.

"Remember how sunburned he got?"

Alfredo nods. "His skin peeled for weeks!"

Maybe these stories don't sound all that glamorous, the **deer** and the **elevator** and the **SUNBURN**, but wow, do I want to be part of them. Maybe next year, I'll tell a rookie all about how I, Tommy Thompson, farted so loud in Myrtle Beach I made a lifeguard blush.

At some point during the seventh inning, tiny footsteps sound on the stairs, and we turn to see

Kessie peering through the rails. Alfredo's sister is spying on us.

"GET OUT OF HERE!" Alfredo says. He jumps up, grabs a few stuffed baseballs from a box of toys, and throws one in her direction.

"AHHH!" Kessie runs up the stairs, shrieking.

"You're so *mean!*" Diesel says to Alfredo.

"You try living with her!" Alfredo says, taking a seat while holding the remaining stuffed baseballs.

Coach Payne comes downstairs, completely oblivious to his kids arguing, and hands out popcorn. Diesel and Pel share a bowl because it's one of those flirty things to do. I munch on a handful that I took from Goetz.

The Bulldogs talk about school in the fall—what homerooms they'll have, what their teachers will be like, and if the middle school cafeteria will have tostadas on the menu this year or not. No one wants Mr. Burt for math because he's grumpy. And everyone hopes to get Mrs. Galen for science because she lets you chew gum in class. I get in a few words, but no one really listens to me.

When I finish my popcorn, I lean over to grab a napkin and my butt **POPS** out of the small chair like a cork out of a bottle. I edge forward, bump my head against a table, and fall to the floor on my back.

"You all right, bro?" Alfredo asks. He leans over me, looking like a young, beardless, sunglasses-free version of his dad.

"Should we put him into concussion protocol?" Goetz asks.

Everyone starts laughing, even Diesel.

"Sorry," Diesel says. "Concussions aren't funny."

Pel makes eyes at her as if she's some kind of angel. **GAG**.

I jump up and squeeze my butt back into the rocking chair, pretending like everything is perfect. But all I can think about are the ten million reasons I'm not going to be a Bulldog.

Alfredo throws two baseballs across the room, connecting one with his sister, who's spying on us again. It hits her arm softly, and she dashes back upstairs.

"You are a *monster*!" Diesel says to Alfredo, half jokingly. She turns toward the staircase and hollers, "Kessie—you can come down here!"

Kessie takes a few steps down the stairs and peers through the railing again.

"Come sit with us," Diesel says.

Kessie thinks about it. Then she darts down the stairs, jumps next to Diesel's lap, and lets her brother know what she thinks about him.

"I saw you at my practice," Kessie says to me. "What's your name?"

"Tommy."

"Thompson?"

"That's right."

She turns to Pel. "And you're the Penguin, right?"

"Pelican," Pel replies.

Kessie glances back and forth between us. "My dad says one of you is gonna get the spot on the team."

The room goes silent. And I can tell by Alfredo's look that what Kessie just said is true.

"KESSIE—GET OUT OF HERE!" Alfredo's booming voice shakes the room, and Kessie is out of the basement before I can blink.

I sit up, ready to launch out of the rocking chair and through the roof. "What's she talking about?"

Alfredo shrugs. "Beats me."

"Tell us!" Diesel says. "You know something!"

Alfredo stares across the basement, seemingly lost in thought. After what feels like forever, he says, "Look—if I tell you guys, you better keep your big mouths shut."

Everyone leans forward in their seats. Except me, because I ended up on the floor the last time I tried that.

"Kessie overheard my dad talking to Coach Decker. They're cutting three people, which leaves six."

"Seven," I say.

"Huh?"

"If they cut three people, that leaves seven."

"Whatever," Alfredo says. "It doesn't really matter because my dad and Decker are really only interested in two players—**you and Pel**."

I'm sure I must have heard wrong. What Alfredo really said was, *My dad and Decker think you'd be better off with the Rainbow Butterflies.*

Pel and I lock gazes. I have no idea what he's thinking.

"You can't tell *anyone*," Alfredo says. "I *mean* it."

"WOW," Clutch says. She looks at me and Pel. **"ONE OF YOU IS GOING TO BE A BULLDOG."**

I sit there, thinking about it. Then I spring from my chair, startling everyone.

"Dude!" Pits says. "What are you—"

"Where's the bathroom?" I ask.

"Upstairs," Alfredo says. "Second door on the—"

It all feels like a blur. I rush across the basement and take the steps two at a time. In the foyer, I wave to Coach Payne and practically dive out the front door. I march into the middle of the yard to get away from the house. Then I do what I came out here for—I text Pel.

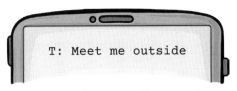

T: Meet me outside

After a few seconds, a text from Pel appears.

P: Everyone thinks you're taking a poop.

I roll my eyes and text again.

T: Dude get out here!!

After what seems like a million years, the front door swings open, and Pel walks over to me.

"So," Pel says. "It's between you and me."

"Yeah—but you're dropping out!"

Pel doesn't respond. And it makes me nervous.

"You're dropping out, right?" I say. "I mean, you *hate* baseball!"

Pel shrugs. "I actually kind of like it."

I try to make sense of things. "Is it baseball you like—or Diesel?"

"Does it matter?" he asks.

"Of *course* it matters! You can't—"

"I like all the Bulldogs!" Pel says. "Even Goetz."

"*Goetz?*"

"He's never been mean to me."

It feels like I'm in a really bad nightmare. I stare at Pel, and he stares at me.

"YOU PROMISED!" I say, feeling the tightness in my eyes. "You promised you'd give up the spot!"

"I never promised that."

"On the first day of tryouts!" I realize how loud my voice is getting, but I can't do anything to quiet it. "When we were standing in the field!"

"I NEVER PROMISED—"

"You did! You promised *me*!"

More silence. I want to say something, but the words feel stuck in my throat. A mix of emotions push against the inside of my chest.

"I'm not giving up," Pel says at last. "I'm sorry, Tommy, but I want to be a Bulldog. I deserve a fair shot."

I shake my head, barely able to believe what I'm hearing. "Baseball's *my* thing! Remember?"

"It's one team, Tommy. There are other options."

"Like what?" I ask. "*Rec ball?*"

"Maybe it's where you fit best."

My hands rise up and push Pel's chest. He stumbles backward, almost falling.

"Seriously?" Pel says. "You're gonna *push* me?"

"The Bulldogs are *my* team—not yours! I've been waiting for this **ALL MY LIFE**!"

"Yeah . . . so have I."

I squish my eyebrows together. "Being a *Bulldog*?"

"No—**fitting in**!" Pel points to the house. "They like me! Alfredo, Diesel, Clutch—even Goetz!"

"Goetz is a—"

"And you know what?" Pel says. "I'm pretty sure Diesel has a crush on me. Do you know how *wild* that is? She's a year older than us and one of the coolest girls I've ever met!"

"Yeah, but—"

"All that stuff—it's **BIGGER** than baseball," Pel says. "It's even **BIGGER** than you and me!"

I feel my face twist up like a balloon animal at a kid's party. The thought that anything could be more important than our friendship is devastating.

"You want the spot on the team?" Pel says. "Then *earn* it! I'm showing up tomorrow, and I'm bringing my A game." He turns and marches to the house.

"Pel—*wait!*"

He steps onto the porch, opens the door, and goes inside, returning to his new friends. I look up and see Coach Payne watching from the window. I'm not sure how long he was looking, but when our gazes meet, he ducks out of view.

My emotions continue to swirl. Though I'm angry at Pel, a part of me wants to run after him and admit that he deserves the spot on the team—that he's better than me at baseball, and at video games, and at a lot of things. And maybe I don't always see it, but he fits in with me.

Lacking the courage for any of that, I pick up my bike and wipe away the wetness in my eyes. Then I take off down the road, trying to escape the feeling that I'm **losing everything.**

Chapter 24
Persistent Payne

I stand at the top of the basement stairs. It feels like my friendship with Tommy just ended.

"You okay?"

A familiar voice pulls me out of my thoughts. Coach Payne stands in the kitchen, looking at me.

"Huh?" I say. It's the only word I can find.

"Maybe you should go after him," Coach says.

I stare at him, wishing I could see his eyes instead of his dark sunglasses.

Coach Payne crosses his arms and leans backward, resting his rear end against the bottom cabinets. He tips his head to the side, gesturing to the front yard. "Your friend Tommy. Maybe you should go get him. **Some things are more important than baseball**."

I sort through my thoughts and seem to find the one that matters most. "**This isn't about baseball, Coach**."

Coach Payne stares at me, his eyes concealed by the dark lenses. "Okay," he says at last. "I get it."

I wait for him to say something more. Something that will help me make sense of everything. Something wise. But he only stands with his arms crossed, frowning.

I nod at him. Then I turn and head back downstairs.

Chapter 25
Practicing with Pete

After leaving the Dog Pound, I headed straight for Wurtmore Park. Coach Payne keeps a couple tees and a bucket of balls in the dugout. Now the park is empty except for a few kids on the playground.

I place a ball on the tee, get into my stance, and swing. It's a weak grounder into the backstop.

"Stupid baseball," I mutter under my breath.

Baseball isn't the only thing that feels stupid at the moment. **Everything** does.

I tee up another ball. My arms are tired because I've been at this for at least an hour. I need to get my swing right for the last day of tryouts. Pel's already won the Bulldog popularity contest, so I need to beat him on the field.

Another ball, another swing, another weak grounder. I haven't hit this bad in years!

"Tommy?" I hear a familiar voice say.

It's Pete.

I watch as Pete rides up the sidewalk on a motorized scooter. He's wearing a sparkly red helmet and plastic sunglasses with blue frames. A wire basket on the front of the scooter is filled with empty pickle jars. He veers onto the field and pulls up near me. I blink ONCE, TWICE, THREE times.

"You have a scooter," I say at last.

"I do."

"And a bunch of empty pickle jars."

Pete nods.

"I'm working on some pickles at home."

In my experience, people usually work on cars, or computers, or carpentry. I've never heard of anyone *working on* pickles.

"You should shorten your swing," Pete says.

"Huh?"

"Compact it," he adds, and steps off the scooter.

He positions his arms like he's holding a bat and demonstrates the first half of a typical swing. "See my elbow? Close to the body, not"—he extends his arms—"out here."

I can't believe I'm getting baseball tips from a guy who sells pickles for a living.

"Quick swing," he says, "straight to the ball."

When it's obvious I have no idea what he's talking about, Pete takes the bat and puts a ball on the tee. "Shorten your stride—just a shift of your weight, really." He demonstrates what he's talking about and hands me the bat. "You try."

I do, barely making contact. The ball rolls weakly against the backstop again.

"Your swing's still too long." He grabs another ball from the bucket and sets it up. "Your elbows should be close to your body."

I have no idea if it's good advice. But when I swing this time, the ball CRASHES into the backstop and **rattles** the chain-link fence.

"See that?" Pete says. "Nice and compact, all the way to your launch position."

"How do you know so much about baseball?" I ask.

He winks and sets up another ball. "Try again. Stay connected to the bat."

I square up to the tee and line another shot into the backstop.

"Bravo!" Pete says. "Now try some more."

He loads *ANOTHER* ball on the tee—and *ANOTHER* and *ANOTHER.* I keep pounding them, and before I know it, we've had to refill the bucket at least a dozen times. He gives me tips on things like turning my wrists and planting my feet.

"And you don't need to spit so much," he says at one point. "You'll dehydrate."

After fifteen minutes, we pause to catch our breath. I notice the empty jars on the scooter again.

"How did you get into pickling?" I ask Pete. "Did you go to college for that?"

Pete laughs even though it wasn't a joke. "My parents farmed cucumbers," he says. "Pickling was something I used to do for fun. I didn't start selling pickles until the Wurtmore County Fair opened about fifty years ago."

"What was Wurtmore like back then?"

"Slower, for sure," he says. "People had more time to reflect on things."

"Hmm." The only time I reflect on anything for more than five seconds is when I lose my Wi-Fi connection. "Did you have a lot of friends?"

"I'm not sure I had a lot of *anything*. Cucumbers, I guess. But friends don't grow like cucumbers, and they're hard to come by when you live on a grassy plain."

Pete's always saying smart stuff like that. He must read a lot when he's not pickling.

"But you know what?" he asks. "Not having a lot of friends is what makes the friends you *do* have special." He pauses. "Where's Pel? I thought you two were attached at the hip."

"Guess not."

"You're both trying out for the Bulldogs, aren't you?"

I nod.

"I heard there's only one spot on the team," he says. "I'm sure it'll be hard for you if Pel makes the team and you don't. Or vice versa. Can I offer some advice?"

"Sure."

"JUST DO YOUR BEST," he says. "Not only with baseball but as a friend."

I smile, feeling weird about the way Pete always knows what's going on inside me.

Pete claps his hand on my shoulder and says, "I should go. Those jars aren't going to fill themselves with brine."

"Thanks, Pete."

He climbs onto his scooter and says, "Compact your swing. Stay inside the ball. Be a good friend."

Words to live by. I can practically see them on a plaque.

Compact your swing.
Stay inside the ball.
Be a good friend.
  -Pete
Founder of Pete's Pickles

Pete salutes me like a soldier. Combined with his helmet, his scooter, and his empty pickle jars, it might be the strangest thing I've ever seen, but somehow, it works.

"See ya, Pete."

"It's **au revoir** and not goodbye!"

I smile, watching the owner of Pete's Pickles ride off into the sunset. Then I pick up a ball and set it on the tee.

The last day of tryouts is closing in. And I have a *lot* to practice.

Chapter 26
Pel and Miguel

I turn my bike off the street and pedal up the driveway. Miguel and Alejandra are playing catch in the yard with the remaining summer light before sunset, and Mom is sitting on the porch about thirty feet away, sipping her evening tea.

"How'd it go?" Mom asks.

"Good." I set my bike down in the grass. "The Bulldogs are really nice."

"You seem surprised," she says.

I shrug one shoulder. I *am* surprised.

"Did you eat?" she asks.

I nod. "Pizza."

Miguel throws the ball **HIGH**. It sails over Alejandra and rolls to a stop near my feet. I pick it up and give it a **squeeze**. It's one of those rubbery balls that little kids use when they're just starting out. I walk over and stand beside Alejandra.

"Teach him how to throw," Alejandra says. "He's not doing it right."

"Like this," I say to Miguel. I turn my body sideways and square up to him. "Point your glove at your target"—I show him what I mean—"and throw."

I lob the ball to Miguel, who reaches out his glove but doesn't come close to making the catch.

"Good try," I say.

Miguel smiles at the compliment and runs over to pick up the ball.

"You throw better than him," Alejandra whispers to me.

I grin. "That's because I'm older."

Miguel hurries back to his former spot and throws the ball without doing a thing that I suggested. As the ball flies over Alejandra's head, I reach out my glove and catch it. Mom cheers.

"**BETTER,**" I say, even though the throw might have been worse. "But remember to turn your body"—I square up to him again—"**like this.**" I make another throw, slowly going through my motions to demonstrate. This time, the ball bounces off his glove.

I glance toward the porch and see Mom smiling. When she notices my attention, she winks at me.

"Pel!" Miguel says, and I turn just in time to catch another errant throw. But Miguel is squared up to me this time, at least a little.

"Nice," I say, pointing my glove at him the same way Diesel points to Torque after a good pitch. The Bulldogs are already rubbing off on me. I wonder how different I might be after a season.

"Here," I say, and hand the ball to Alejandra. "You try."

She turns so one hip is facing Miguel and points her glove at her target.

"Like this?" she asks, standing statue-still.

"Perfect," I say. Alejandra has always been a quick learner.

She steps forward and pitches her arm around. The ball sails through the air—

—and lands in Miguel's open glove.

"Yay!" Mom says. She sets down her tea and claps her hands, her red fingernails flashing in the evening light.

Miguel smiles and holds his glove above his head. I'm not sure I've seen him looking so proud. And I feel proud, too, realizing I had something to do with it.

"Nice catch, Miguel!" I say.

He jumps around until the ball pops out of his mitt and bounces off his head. When Mom laughs, Alejandra and I join her.

For a second, everything is **wonderful** in a way I can't explain. It's like I never had a fight with Tommy. There's just **THIS MOMENT** and **the importance I have to my family**.

Chapter 27
The Bulldog Brawl

"You excited, Tommy?" Dad asks from his seat behind the wheel. Ma is sitting on the passenger side, and I'm in the seat right behind her.

"I've been ready for this **my whole life**." It's true, but even I can hear the lack of confidence in my voice.

"You made it this far," Ma says. "No matter what happens today, you should be proud."

I nod, but I don't believe it. I'll be proud once I'm a Bulldog.

Dad turns onto Chester Lane and drives through downtown. We get caught in the traffic for what feels like days and finally coast into the parking lot surrounding Wurtmore Park. Hundreds of lawn chairs are set up along the sidelines; people are grilling, playing cornhole, and lying in the grass to catch some rays before the Bulldog Brawl begins. It's super-hot out, and the bleachers are packed.

I jump out of the car as soon as Dad parks it and run toward the field. **"See ya!"**

"HAVE FUN!" Dad calls out as he and Ma head for the bleachers.

Having fun is the last thing on my mind, of course. All I care about is making the team.

As I near the dugout, Kessie walks up to me in dusty ballet slippers and a pink tutu. She demonstrates a few ballet moves that include the plié and the relevé. I can tell she's been practicing because she actually looks a little better at it than before. Then she scurries away.

I drop my backpack in the dugout, pull out my mitt, and head onto the field, feeling nervous. Two umpires are talking near home plate. It's the first time in tryouts that we've had officiating.

I survey the Bulldogs. Pel is warming up with Diesel, which is nothing new, I guess. Coach Decker is catching for Torque, Alfredo is eating a snack, and Goetz is leaning against the fence, chumming around with a couple of his buddies in the crowd.

I stretch for a few moments and then head over to Pel. I should apologize for yesterday, maybe even wish him good luck. But when Pel sees me coming, he heads to the bench.

"*Whatever,*" I say under my breath.

A bunch of adults start a line dance when a country song begins to play. Ma screams—with excitement, it seems—and joins them. Two seconds later, she's moving in perfect sync with everyone around her: **step, step, kick, step, wobble, wobble**.

It's weird to see her having so much fun but also kinda cool. Note to self—ask Ma for dancing lessons before my eighth-grade prom.

"All right!" Coach Payne says after a few minutes. "Bring it in!"

We do, and he divides us into teams. Pel and I end up opposite each other. As Pel's team takes the field, *THE MUSIC STOPS*, disappointing the line dancers, and the crowd settles in.

Coach Decker grabs a clipboard and calls out the batting order. I'm first to hit. As I make my way onto the field, the head umpire yells, **"BALLS IN!"** and writes something on a lineup card. Serious stuff. You'd think this was game seven of the World Series or something.

Diesel catches the last warm-up pitch, springs to her feet, and throws down to second, where Naeem Taylor applies the tag to an imaginary runner. As I step into the batter's box, Diesel winks at me and says, "You ready?"

I am, at least a little. But it isn't easy playing for such a huge crowd, especially with so much on the line.

"Be a hitter!" comes a familiar voice.

I look up and smile at Pete, who's sitting nearby in the bleachers.

Diesel squats behind the plate and holds up her mitt as a target. Torque nods to show that she's ready. Then she takes a deep breath, rolls her shoulders, and delivers a fastball, high and tight. I lean back, and the ball whistles by me.

I back up and take a few practice swings, glad that my head is still intact. Then I return to my spot and get ready for the next pitch. When it comes, I swing and totally whiff.

As Diesel tosses the ball back, I try not to think about the crowd, the noise, and how important this moment is. The next pitch is low and inside, and the pitch after that catches the inside corner.

"**STEEEE-RIKE!**" the ump calls. It gets the crowd fired up, and a few infielders clap their hands against their mitts.

I swing one foot out of the box and take a deep breath. My gaze happens upon Pel in right field. It's weird that he's rooting against me.

"Let's go, batter," the ump says, because I'm taking too long.

I step back into position, bend my knees, and think of everything Pete showed me. I batted balls against the backstop last night until it was too dark to see.

Torque leans forward, staring at her target. Then she stands straight and goes into motion, delivering the next pitch.

I swing, keeping the barrel close to my body, and target the inside of the ball. The bat connects with a **CRACK!**, and I line a shot into center field.

I drop my bat and take off for first base.

Coach Payne waves me to second and says, **"GO! GO! GO!"**

First base is beneath my cleats and then behind me. I look up to see the center fielder bobble the ball.

Second base is ten strides away, maybe fewer. Two seconds later, I pound the bag and head for third, knowing the throw will be close. I slide head-first, barely beating the tag, and the crowd explodes with applause.

I rise, covered in dust and feeling like a warrior.

I take it all in. The crowd, the players, Pete, my parents. Pel stares at me, his glove at his side and his mullet blowing. It feels like we're cowboys at a high-noon showdown.

It's the final day of tryouts for the Bulldogs. And I'm not going **down** without a fight.

Chapter 28
Pel's Three-Bagger

Alfredo walks right past me in the dugout and says, **"Looks like your boy came to PLAY!"**

He's talking about Tommy's leadoff triple, his best hit of the tryouts. Tommy's team scored two runs, and now it's our turn to do some damage.

"BALLS IN!"

I grab my bat and head onto the field. A Bulldog named Trey Williams is pitching, and Goetz, the backup catcher for Diesel, is behind the plate.

As I step into the batter's box, Goetz says, "Five bucks you can't hit the Turd Tank again."

"Ten bucks says I'm gonna try."

I glance at my family in the stands, hoping to draw some inspiration. Mom is clapping; Miguel and Alejandra are standing on a seat midway up the bleachers. The three of them are smiling and looking nervous at the same time. I try to remember the last time I saw them together like this. I can't. Maybe it was for Dad?

Williams stands sideways on the mound, his foot against the rubber. I take a look at the first pitch, which comes in high. The next pitch is in the dirt, and the count jumps to 2−0. It's called a hitter's count, because the pitcher is likely to put the next ball in the strike zone to avoid walking the batter. I know because Diesel told me.

Williams stands with his chin on his shoulder and stares at Goetz's glove, his target. I let the next pitch go by and the ump calls, **"STEEEE-RIKE!"**

I step out of the box and look around, upset with the call. Spectators are sitting in lawn chairs, in the bleachers, and on the roofs of cars. Teenagers are hanging out in groups, and children are flying kites. The Turd Tank looms beyond center field, daring anyone to come near it.

No one does.

Tommy stands in left field, the brim of his cap pulled low. An out here would make his triple feel like a home run.

"Batter—you ready?"

I step back into the box and get ready for the 2–1 pitch. When it comes, I **BLAST** it with the sweet part of the bat.

The crowd **CHEERS** as I tear down the first baseline. The ball shoots past the diving reach of the center fielder, and a few air horns blow. As I round first base, my mind is on one thing, and that's getting to third, like Tommy.

I spring off second base and blow past the kid trying out at shortstop. Coach Decker signals for me to stay at third, and it's a stand-up triple.

The crowd erupts again, and people jump out of their chairs. Never in a million years would I expect a scrimmage to have so much energy.

I call time and step off the base to tighten my shoelaces. Then I stand straight again and lock gazes with Tommy.

We turn our attention back to the game, which is far from being over.

Chapter 29
The Last Inning

I drop my glove, plop on the bench, and grab my water bottle. ***GLUG! GLUG! GLUG!***

I take off my hat and wipe my dusty forearm against my brow. We're up by a run at the end of the fourth inning, and Pel's team is warming up on the field.

As the rowdy crowd breaks out with the wave, a man who is Dad's age falls out of his chair and spills whatever was in his red plastic cup all over him. Everyone breaks out in laughter as he stands up to take a bow.

The mood on the field isn't quite so festive, because we're all playing to win. I'm two for three at the plate and made a diving catch in left field. Pel has only one hit—the triple in the first inning—and he failed to catch a routine pop-up, which caused two runners to score. I've played better than he has, and I'm sure the coaches have noticed.

"BALLS IN!" the ump shouts.

As the fifth and final inning starts, I realize my stomach isn't feeling so good. Maybe it's nerves. Maybe it's what Ma and Pete warned me about— that fiber makes you poop.

The first batter hits a grounder to Clutch, who scoops up the ball and throws to first for the easy out.

From right field, I stare into the stands and find my family again. Mom is locked in on the baseball action, and Miguel and Alejandra have their faces buried in pink clouds of cotton candy.

As the next batter steps to the plate, my gaze passes along the opposing team's bench, and I spot Tommy.

Something seems wrong with him.

After three quick outs, we're back on the field. It's the bottom of the last inning, with our team still up by a run. Pits is at the plate, and I don't wanna admit it, but I have to go to the bathroom something **FIERCE**. My stomach aches, and all I can think about is the twenty-three bags of sunflower seeds that I ate. I look over at the Turd Tank, and the nasty thing winks at me.

The Turd Tank knows what I know. Out here in the field, it's my only option for relief.

But first I need to finish the game—to **win**, to **BEAT PEL**, to *get that spot on the team*.

Calling a time-out for a toilet break in front of a thousand people and entering the grossest porta-potty known to mankind isn't something I want to do. We just need three outs.

Pits lines the first pitch into right field for a single, and Tower steps up to the plate, taking his sweet time. Williams gets the ball back and strolls around the mound, as if casually contemplating life.

"LET'S GO, WILLIAMS!" I shout—not to encourage him but to speed him along.

Williams looks my way, confused. Then he takes his position and delivers the next pitch, and Tower fouls one off into the crowd.

I grab my belly, which just lurched again.

It's going to be a long, painful inning.

"Check out your boy," Alfredo says to me. "What's he doing?"

Tommy is leaning forward, grimacing. After a few seconds, he stands up straight, takes off his hat, and uses his forearm to wipe his brow.

"I THINK HE'S GOTTA POOP," I say.

Alfredo cracks up. Then he says, "Aww, man—this is gonna be good!"

Alfredo might be right but not in ways he meant. If I can hit the ball into left field the next time I'm up to bat, Tommy might not be able to field it. And that extra hit might be enough for the coaches to pick me over him.

Tommy takes about five steps to one side and leans over, clutching his stomach. Then he returns to his former spot and leans backward this time, hands on his hips.

"Look at him!" Alfredo says. **"He's not gonna make it!"**

Tower *finally* gets a piece of the ball and sends a slow grounder to third. It advances the runner, but

Deion Wright, a kid trying to make the team, throws to first, and it's one out.

The Turd Tank beckons to me. I want to run to it, throw open the door, and sacrifice myself to whatever **horror** lives inside. It's amazing what stomach cramps can do to a person's psyche.

Alfredo strolls up to the plate and takes about five hundred practice swings before stepping into the box. I've only seen Alfredo connect with the ball a few times, so I'm guessing there's a ninety-nine percent chance he'll strike out. I just need Williams to put three quick pitches into the strike zone.

The first pitch is a ball.

The second pitch is a ball.

The third pitch is a ball.

You gotta be kidding me.

"C'MON, WILLIAMS!" I shout.

Williams puts the next two pitches into the strike zone and loads the count. Alfredo gets a piece of the sixth pitch, and the ball sails out of bounds, nearly clipping a few people in the stands.

I buckle with a fresh cramp. It's all I can do not to drop my mitt and run for the Turd Tank.

"THOMPSON!" Coach Payne hollers. **"YOU ALL RIGHT?"**

I manage to stand up straight and hold a thumb in the air.

Alfredo gets a piece of the next pitch, and the ball goes foul. The Turd Tank continues to call for me.

After another foul tip—you gotta be kidding me—Alfredo finally goes down swinging.

Two outs, a runner on, and Pel struts to the plate.

I stand outside the batter's box, take a few practice swings, and stare into left field. Tommy looks worse than ever.

I must be grimacing, because Goetz says, "What's so funny?"

"Nothing," I say.

I tap my cleats with my bat . . .

. . . and pull up my socks . . .

. . . and adjust my batting glove.

"C'MON, BATTER!" Tommy shouts, his voice booming across the field.

I smile and take my time, adjusting my pants, my shirt, my batting helmet. I take a step away from the plate instead of toward it.

"LET'S GO!" Tommy hollers.

I grin. The longer I stall, the worse it gets for Tommy. And the better my chances get at driving a ball past him.

I can't believe what I'm seeing. I don't need the *Wurtmore Parks Youth Sport Manual* to know that hitters can't take this long to get ready.

Pel **SLOOOOWLY** steps up to the plate and then he **SLOOOOWLY** gets ready for the next pitch. Pel can take his time, sure, but I've never seen him move like this in my life!

And that's when it finally hits me.

He's doing this on purpose.

The first pitch is out of the strike zone, and I let it go by. Then I step out of the box to stretch a few muscles.

"All right, kid," the umpire says. He points toward the plate and adds, "Let's play some ball already."

I casually stroll up to the plate and take my time getting ready for the next pitch.

I'M NOT GOING TO MAKE IT!

Pel takes another ball, then swings and misses on the next pitch. The count jumps to 2–1. He rubs his eye like he's got something in it—a gnat, maybe. But when Pel holds up his hand to request a time-out, I know the gnat isn't real.

"TIME!" the ump yells. His arms are up in the air like he's on the first hill of a roller coaster.

Pel walks around, still rubbing his eye, and Coach Payne jogs over to check on him. I can hardly believe what I'm seeing.

"LET'S PLAY SOME BALL!" I shout.

My teammates stare at me like I'm the rudest guy in the world. At the moment, I might be.

After what feels like forever, Coach Payne claps Pel on the back and gets off the field. Pel steps back into the box. He misses the next pitch, and the count jumps to 2–2. That's when a horrifying thought strikes me. If Pel gets on base, the game's not over.

The next out is even more important than I thought.

My stomach growls again.

The pitch comes in so high that Goetz has to reach over his head to catch it.

"FULL COUNT!" the ump shouts.

As Goetz tosses the ball back to the pitcher, I step out of the box again. Williams strolls around the mound, probably to catch his breath, and the crowd cheers louder than ever. If I can get ahold of the next pitch—maybe find a gap in the outfield— it'll be game over.

"BATTER—LET'S GO!" the ump calls out.

I step one foot in the box and grip the bat with both hands. A swing and miss right now might give Tommy the place on the team, but it could also **SAVE OUR FRIENDSHIP.**

That unexpected thought startles me. A part of me can't imagine life without Tommy. We're supposed to be best friends until the end. We made that promise when we first met, so many years ago. Now it's like we're enemies. I can't have that.

"Batter—you okay?" the ump asks.

I nod, even though I'm not.

"Then let's go!"

I take a deep breath and settle into the stance that Diesel taught me. I think of Tommy again: our walks to school, our sleepovers, our bike rides around town. He's like a brother to me, but a brother with a bad side. How many times has he told me I'm not good enough at sports, at school, at making new friends? How many times has he made fun of me?

"Too many," I say under my breath.

"Huh?" Goetz says, thinking I'm talking to him.

Williams goes into his movement, and when the pitch comes, I swing as hard as I can.

CCRRAAACKKK!!!

As the ball rockets to the left-center gap, Pits and I take off running.

I sprint for the ball, which looks like it's going to drop between me and the center fielder, Drake Robinson, another kid who's trying out. I run like everything is A-OK with my body, but I'm really about two seconds away from the embarrassment of a lifetime.

The ball descends with me and Robinson **RUNNING** and **RUNNING** and **RUNNING.** The crowd explodes because they know this could be the final play of the game.

Robinson stumbles and face-plants in the grass just left of center.

Laughter mixes with the cheers, my guts get ready to burst, and the ball continues to **FALL . . .**

. . . AND FALL . . .

. . . AND FALL . . .

I stretch out my arm, pushing through my pain. Realizing the ball is out of reach, I dive over Robinson.

It's an epic moment for sure, regardless of how it ends.

The ball lands in my mitt—

 —and **POPS** back out when I hit the ground.

I round second and head for third while Tommy and Robinson lie in the field. There's no chance for a throw to reach the plate before I do.

I jump up, drop my mitt, and run for deep center field.

The crowd cheers, and I hardly **HEAR IT**.

The sun beats down, and I hardly **FEEL IT**.

Pel is going to win, and I hardly care.

I throw open the door and step into what has haunted Wurtmore Park since forever.

THE
TURD TANK

Chapter 30
POOP! There It Is!

Rounding third base, I look into center field. Robinson is getting to his feet, but there's no Tommy. When I see this—

—I realize what's happening.

"Six! Seven! Eight!" chants the crowd. They're counting how many seconds Tommy has been in the Turd Tank.

I touch home plate and get a few high fives from the other players as they step onto the field. They're interested in Tommy right now, not me.

Light filters through the dusty screens along the top of the Turd Tank—vents that do nothing to clear the air of the horrible smell. The toilet looks like a bucket with the bottom punched out. I glance into the pit and can hardly believe what's in there.

I hold the top of my shirt over my mouth and nose like a mask. It reminds me of all my **KHOOOOH PUUUHRR** moments in the past few days.

When I drop the lid with my foot, the **BANG** makes me jump.

I reach for toilet paper to cover the seat, but there's not much left—

—and I'll need that for something more important.

I drop my pants and take a seat, forgetting that I'm wearing my cup. I jump up, correct everything, and sit back down without a second to spare. My insides open in surprising ways, and the noise is like a tuba in an echo chamber.

The pain in my stomach subsides, and I wait a second to see if it'll come back. Then I hear the crowd laughing and cheering and . . . *counting*?

"Thirty-five! Thirty-six! Thirty-seven!"

What in the world are they doing? Why would—?

I sit up straight as the answer strikes me.

They're counting to see if I'll beat the record for the longest time spent in the Turd Tank, which is a hundred and thirty-two seconds.

"Forty-three! Forty-four! Forty-five!"

Everyone has joined the count—the players, the coaches, even the two umps.

Diesel walks up, smiles, and nudges me with her elbow. "Where did you *find* this guy?" she asks, meaning Tommy.

I honestly don't know what to say, because Tommy has always been there.

"Fifty-two! Fifty-three! Fifty-four!"

Another wave of pain hits, and I'm pretty sure I'll never eat a sunflower seed again. I notice the graffiti on one wall.

"Sixty! Sixty-one! Sixty-two!"

The smell continues to invade my senses. I can practically see it, like a dark fog. I realize my eyes are watering.

NO SEEDS! (EVER?)

TURD!

Something drops from the ceiling and lands in my pants—a spider with a body like a plump raisin. I scream and kick out my legs, striking the door latch at a weird angle. As the spider scurries off into the shadows, I wonder how anything can live in this horrid stench.

I rip off what's left of the toilet paper from the roll, wad it into a ball, and reach behind me, knowing I have one chance to get this right. Two seconds later, I stand and pull up my pants, struggling to get the athletic cup to fit like it's supposed to.

I try to open the door, but it doesn't budge. **OH NO.** I must have damaged the latch!

"Seventy-two! Seventy-three! Seventy-four!"

I take a few steps onto the field and squint at the Turd Tank. The door is shaking.

"He can't get out," I say to the Bulldogs behind me.

Goetz and Alfredo laugh harder than ever. Diesel walks up next to me for a better look at what's happening.

"Eighty-one! Eighty-two!"

A few Bulldogs clap, and others scramble to get their phones.

The last thing Tommy needs is to break the record for the longest time in the Turd Tank. People say it's why Roy Davis, the current record holder, skipped town with his family.

"Should I help him?" I ask Diesel.

She shrugs. "He's your friend, not mine."

It must be the answer I need to hear because my feet suddenly start moving. By the time I reach the pitcher's mound, I break into a run.

I throw my shoulder against the plastic door, again and again. The door shakes but doesn't open. How can the latch be so messed up?

"C'mon, you stupid thing!"

"Ninety-five! Ninety-six! Ninety-seven!"

I do the math in my head and realize I'm only thirty-six seconds from breaking the record.

"NO! NO! NO!"

I plow my shoulder against the door again, but the latch still doesn't release. It dawns on me that I'm TRAPPED IN **THE TURD TANK**.

I leap over second base and exit the infield, barely aware that the crowd is cheering harder than ever. Do they know what I'm doing?

The outfield grass is a blur beneath my feet. A gnat lands in my eye, and a bigger bug flies into my mouth. I spit it out, and my revulsion kicks me into a higher speed.

"One hundred three! One hundred four!"

Tommy needs me.

The thought makes me realize I need him just as much.

"SOMEONE HELP!"

I'm not sure who I expect that someone to be. Pel is probably celebrating his victory with his new friends, and the crowd is having too much fun.

I accidentally take a deep breath, and the **rancid air** pours into my mouth. Something about the way it tastes like rotted fruit is horrifying.

As I reach to try the latch again, the door suddenly shakes. Someone is outside, trying to help.

"Tommy!" Pel says. "It's me!"

One corner of my mouth curls up with the slightest grin. It's my best friend to the rescue, like so many times before.

"One hundred sixteen! One hundred seventeen!"

Time is running out. And I'm almost certain it will soon be my name replacing Roy Davis's name on the side of the Turd Tank.

"One hundred eighteen! One hundred nineteen!"

"Push, Tommy!" I say.

When I feel his weight against the door, I dig my heels in the dirt and pull as hard as I can. Nothing happens.

"One hundred twenty-three! One hundred twenty-four!"

I plant both palms on the door and push as hard as I can. When sunlight appears along the frame, I realize the plastic door is bowing outward.

"One hundred twenty-eight! One hundred twenty-nine!"

Four seconds until I beat the record.

I lower my arms and lean back as far as I can. Before I can think about what I'm doing, I throw my weight forward like a defensive lineman. The door swings open and—

"ONE THIRTY-THREE!!!"

—I plunge through the opening and crash into Pel. We fall to the ground together.

I lie in the grass beside Tommy. Horns blare and a few small fireworks shoot over the field. Everything feels surreal, like the final moment in a bizarre dream.

"Bro—you all right?" Tommy asks.

I turn my head to see him. He's so close that I can make out a dusty cobweb in his hair.

"Shouldn't I be asking you that question?" I say.

Tommy smiles, and we roll our heads to look toward the sky again. Another firework goes off, and red sparks shoot across the field. I smell something horrid and think that it's Tommy. But it's the Turd Tank. The broken door is gaped open, and the stench from the pit is wafting outside.

"WAY TO GO, TOMMY TWICE!" Goetz shouts.

The crowd erupts in laughter, then begins a new chant. It takes a moment for their voices to sync.

"TOM-MY TWICE!! TOM-MY TWICE!!"

As the chant gets louder, I turn to look at Tommy, worried about the way he'll react.

I get to one knee, the putrid smell of the Turd Tank still in my nose. Then I stand up, aware that my pants are practically on sideways. My athletic cup is a few inches from where it needs to be, but right now certainly isn't the time to fix it.

"TOM-MY TWICE!! TOM-MY TWICE!!"

I pause, thinking about everything. Pel will get his name in the Bulldogs' lineup, and I'll get my name on the side of the Turd Tank. Both of our futures are forever changed.

"TOM-MY TWICE!! TOM-MY TWICE!!"

I grin at Pel, and with no clear way to escape the moment, I decide to own it instead.

Half of the Bulldogs charge across the field, waving their arms in the air. More fireworks go off, and the crowd continues to cheer.

"Only you, Tommy!" Pel says as he stands with a smile.

The Bulldogs surround us. My feet shoot off the ground as I'm hoisted into the air, and my rear end lands on the shoulders of Pits and Diesel. Pel is lifted the same way by Torque and Tower.

"Way to go, Fart Boy!" Goetz shouts.

Everyone breaks out laughing.

"Fart Boy" is a teeny, *tiny* bit better than "Fart Vader." I'll take it.

The Bulldogs carry Pel and me toward the infield, where we're surrounded by the other players, all cheering and holding their fists in the air. I look into the stands and find my parents. They're laughing and clapping, faces full of surprise. I glance around until I locate Pete. He's standing tall, saluting me for a reason that hardly seems odd given his personality. I touch two fingers to my brow, returning the gesture.

"TOM-MY TWICE!! TOM-MY TWICE!!"

A Bulldog makes a fart noise, and everyone starts laughing. More players get in on the action, and I recognize the Putter, the BATHTUB, the SONIC BOOM.

The sound effects aren't bad, but everyone could use some practice.

Chapter 31
A Decision to Make

I sit on the end of the empty bench, sipping a cup of water. At least a half hour has passed since my **history-making event** in the Turd Tank. Pete is back at his store, and most of the remaining crowd, including my parents, have moved on to the pubs and restaurants in town, which is part of the Bulldog Brawl tradition. Most of the players are gone too. The ones remaining—Diesel and Pel and their usual crew—are gathered around home plate. Pel's siblings, Miguel and Alejandra, are with him.

Pel strolls over to me and sits down on the bench. "What was it like?" he asks.

"Huh?"

"The Turd Tank," he says.

Grotesque images flash in my mind:

I shudder. "Let's just say I feel bad for whoever breaks my record."

Pel laughs and swats the side of my leg.

"You played good," I add. "That shot to left-center—no way I was getting to that."

"Thanks, man."

"You're a natural," I say. "Not just at baseball but a lot of things." I nod toward Miguel and Alejandra. "They're lucky to have a brother like you."

Pel smiles, looking pleased in a way I'm not accustomed to.

"I'm sorry," I add, the words just falling from my mouth.

Pel focuses on me. "About what?"

I shrug. "A lot of things, I guess. I'm sorry I wasn't a better friend."

"I'm not perfect either," Pel says. "I'm sorry too."

Diesel jogs over and smacks Pel's arm. "You coming or what?" she asks. "And how about you, **TOMMY TWICE**? You up for some ice cream?"

"No chance. After what I saw in there"—I nod at the Turd Tank—"I might not have an appetite for a *week*."

Pel holds out his knuckles for a fist bump and says, "See ya later, Tominator," goofing around with another nickname.

I tap Pel's knuckles. "Tominator?"

"Like the Terminator," he says. "Only with *Tom*."

He's talking about that movie with the cyborg from the future. Great movie, at least the parts my parents let me watch, and it's not a bad nickname. I can totally see myself saying, "You're *Tominated*," after hitting my tenth grand slam or something.

THE
TOMINATOR

Pel mimics the serious look on Arnold Schwarzen*whatever*'s face and says, "Hasta la vista, baby." Well played—it's a big moment in the sequel.

"See ya, guys," I say.

Pel and Diesel walk off, playfully hip-bumping each other. It's gross to watch, but I'm getting pretty used to it. Miguel and Alejandra hurry to catch up to them.

"Later, Turdly!" Goetz says to me.

Another nickname. Hopefully this one doesn't stick.

The group disappears from view altogether. It might be the first time I've truly seen Pel fit in with anyone other than me. And even though it's what *I* wanted . . . it makes me happy.

"Thompson!" Coach Payne calls out. "Can you give me a hand?" He's carrying about ten things, one with each finger, and the team duffel bag is strapped across his back.

"No problem." I grab the cooler and follow him to his vehicle, a rusty pickup with a bumper sticker that says all you need to know about his perspective on life.

Coach Payne starts throwing things into the back of the truck. "Is the Turd Tank as bad as they say?"

I shake my head. **"WORSE."**

"You want some advice?" He tosses the duffel bag into the truck. "Lay off the sunflower seeds."

"Yeah, thanks."

Coach Payne smiles. "How long you been playing rec ball, Thompson?"

"About six years."

"And you had Coach Bryer for three of those, right?"

"Something like that," I say.

"I called Bryer last night. He said he's never coached anyone who loves the game so much."

I stand a little straighter, wondering where Coach Payne's going with this.

"I've been playing ball for *thirty-one years*," he adds. "Started when I was Kessie's age, hitting off the tee."

It's hard to imagine Coach Payne being so young. But it's easy to imagine him dominating the league.

"I played college ball and spent a year in the minors. If it hadn't been for a bad shoulder, I might've had a shot at the big leagues."

None of this surprises me.

"I love the game." He leans toward me and claps my shoulder. "Like you."

I hold my breath, still unsure where this is going.

"I want you to play for me, Thompson."

And just like that, the offer is out there. I can hardly believe it. "What about Pel?"

"He's good, for sure. But he doesn't have your **PASSION** for the game."

I have no idea how to respond, and my feelings are a jumbled mess.

"What do you say, kid?"

I think about how awesome life as a Bulldog would be—**THE BUS RIDES**, *the hotels,*

THE TOURNAMENTS. Then I think about Pel hanging out with Alfredo and Goetz and the rest of the team, FiNALLY FiTTiNG iN. I picture him slipping a jersey over his head for the first time and standing at the plate with the tying run in scoring position.

Coach Payne raises an eyebrow above his sunglasses. "Well?"

"Give it to Pel."

He leans back, as if my words are hanging in the air and he needs a better look at them.

"Give it to Pel," I say again. **"He deserves it more than me."**

"Don't you want to play—"

"I do," I say. "But there's something that means more to me."

Coach Payne crosses his arms and takes some time to process everything. "You sure about this?"

"Yeah, I'm sure." It's true, at least for the moment.

"Pel's lucky to have such a good friend," he says.

"It goes both ways, actually."

Coach Payne claps my shoulder, as if to let me know he's proud of me. Then he climbs into his rusty pickup and looks at me through the open window. I see my reflection in his lenses again.

TOMMY TWICE. Without a travel team, the nickname will never stick.

"Look us up next year," he says, starting the engine. "Maybe we'll have an opening."

He salutes me the way Pete did and drives off across the parking lot. I watch him turn onto the street and disappear on his way into town. Everything feels **SURREAL**. I just gave up something that I once thought was more important than anything. I know better now.

I go back for my mitt and stop to stare at the empty field. I think about Coach Payne, the Turd Tank, and the Rainbow Butterflies. I think of Diesel, Clutch, and Torque. I think of Pel and all the good things that are in store for him.

I smile, **HAPPY AND** SAD **AT THE SAME TIME.** Then I turn and head home, feeling like a part of me is missing.

And like another part of me has been found.

Chapter 32
Pel's First Jersey

"Pel!" Mom calls out from the living room. "You have a visitor!"

I leave my bedroom and hurry down the stairs. Mom and Coach Payne are standing by the sofa.

"Hey, Coach!" I say, stepping across the room. It's strange seeing him in my house.

"Good game today," he says, turning to me. "That stand-up three-bagger—that was nice."

It takes me a moment to realize he's talking about my triple, and I smile to thank him.

Miguel and Alejandra run into the room and suddenly stop when they see Coach Payne.

He's so intimidating that he can have that effect on people.

He holds out a bag to me and says, **"This is for you."**

I must stand there for too long wondering what it could be because Mom tips her head forward, a cue for me to take it. I move in and grab the bag.

"What is it?" Alejandra says as she and Miguel run up beside me.

"I don't know," I say and reach into the bag. My heart rate *JUMPS* as I pull out a baseball jersey.

"It's yours if you want to play," Coach Payne says, one corner of his mouth curled up in a smile.

Mom slaps her hands against her cheeks in surprise.

I look for the right words and can't find them. I flick my gaze between the uniform and Coach Payne.

"Well?" Mom says. "Are you—"

"I'M IN!" I say, nodding my head.

"That's what I'm talking about," Coach Payne says. I lunge forward and wrap my arms around him. The big man hugs me back.

"You did it!" Alejandra says.

I back away from Coach Payne, feeling the warmth in my chest. The good feeling stops when I think about Tommy. This means he didn't make the team.

"You deserve this!" Mom says; she must have a sixth sense or something to know what I'm feeling. "You earned it!"

I smile, but not as brightly as before. It'll be another year of rec league for Tommy.

"Welcome to the team!" Coach Payne says.

Miguel and Alejandra jump in place beside me.

I hold up the jersey to take a look at the front. The team logo isn't what I expected.

"We have a new sponsor," Coach Payne says. "You're the first to know."

I blink a few times. When the logo doesn't change, I crack a smile.

"Pel," Coach Payne says, "can you do me a favor?"

"Of course," I say.

And then I listen to what the favor is.

Chapter 33
The Two Turdles

The doorbell rings a second time, a third time, a fourth. Whoever's out there is just as impatient as Ma. I grunt, grumble, and get off the couch. When I open the front door, Pel is standing there, holding a wrinkled shirt.

"Hey," Pel says.

"Hey." I step onto the porch. Barely three hours have passed since I gave up my spot on the team.

"Check this out," Pel says, tossing me the shirt.

"What is it?" I ask.

"Just check it out."

I hold up the shirt to get a good look.

"What's this?" I ask, thinking I'm looking at the logo for a new rec team.

"We're not the Bulldogs anymore," Pel says. "Bob Dankworth is sponsoring the team this year."

"You gotta be kidding me."

"Hilarious, right?" Pel says. "The Wurtmore Turdles."

"It's not so bad." It's actually **HORRIBLE**, but I'm not about to rain on Pel's parade. I hold out the uniform for him to take.

"It's not mine," he says. "It's yours."

I stare at Pel, confused.

"You made the team," he says.

"Please don't tell me you gave up your spot."

Pel holds out a folded piece of paper. "It's for you."

I unfold it, not knowing what to think.

"Is this a joke?" I ask.

"No joke," Pel says, grinning. "We're gonna be teammates."

I smile the biggest, goofiest smile of my life. Pel and I—**ON THE SAME TEAM**! I study the uniform again. **It isn't so bad**. Of course, **it isn't so good** either.

THOMPSON,
THE LEAGUE GRANTED ME PERMISSION TO CARRY AN ADDITIONAL PLAYER ON MY ROSTER.
TRYOUTS ARE OVER, KID. GET READY FOR THE REAL THING.
— COACH PAYNE

"Check out the back," Pel says. "Coach Payne saved that one for you."

I flip it over.

"Hilarious, right?" Pel says. "You're number two!"

I wipe a tear from the corner of my eye, laughing. Then my thoughts turn serious. "Dude—we better start practicing!"

Pel blinks. "Right now?"

"The season starts next week!"

"But we just—"

"Hold on a sec!" I run inside and hurry to my bedroom. Twenty seconds later, I'm back on the porch with the bucket of bubble gum that I bought from Big Ray's.

"Bubble gum?" Pel says.

"**SERIOUS BALLPLAYERS** blow **serious bubbles**. It's a way to intimidate opposing teams. Plus, there's no fiber in gum. It's great."

Pel stares at me with one eyebrow raised, trying to decide if I'm joking.

I take a seat on the porch bench and pry off the lid. Pel joins me—a little reluctantly, it seems.

"This stuff works best if you can get about ten pieces in your mouth." I drop some onto Pel's lap and add, "Start small—three pieces, maybe—and work your way up. Like with weights." I've never lifted weights in my life, but I'm pretty sure that's how bodybuilders do it. "Ready?"

"I guess so," Pel says.

We chew until the gum gets soft, and then each of us blows a bubble. Pel's is twice the size of mine, and I pretend like it isn't.

"Okay," I say, "let's add a couple pieces."

We do, and the wads of gum make it hard to laugh. I can feel our friendship healing.

More gum and more laughter. The bubbles get **BIGGER** and **BIGGER**—

—and so do the messes they make.

I'm finally a Bulldog—or a Turdle, actually. And having Pel on my team is the best part about it.

Chapter 34
Afterword

The front door opens, and footsteps sound in the foyer. Ma walks into the kitchen and stands next to me at the table. She looks furious.

"What's wrong?" I ask, holding a spoonful of cereal near my mouth.

Ma SCRUNCHES UP HER FACE and manages to look even **ANGRIER**.

"I stopped by Pete's on my way home from work." She holds up a piece of paper. "He gave me this."

"A receipt?" I ask, hopeful.

She holds the paper out to me. "Something like that."

I reluctantly take what's in her hand. Then I flip it over.

"Wow . . ." I say. "Those things really add up! Maybe I can do some chores around the house and—"

"Pete and I already arranged something." She reaches into her tote bag and tosses a cloth garment at me. "Take a look."

I don't want to, but I do anyway. It's an apron—and it's just my size.

"Welcome to your first summer job," Ma says. "You start tomorrow."

Bryan Chick lives in Clarkston, Michigan, with his wife and four kids. When he's not writing or tossing baseballs around, he's usually hanging out with like-minded peers at schools around the nation. A bunch of stuff in *The Super Sports Society* really happened, which goes to show the strange life he's had. A Turd Tank, really? Yes.

When Brett Radlicki is not tripping over his shoelaces during a baseball game, you can find him with a sketchbook creating pictures and comics. Some of these doodles find their way into books, magazines, and garbage cans around the world. *The Super Sports Society* is dear to Brett because of his love for sports, drawing, and portable toilets.

Thank you!

We would like to express sincere gratitude to our families. They patiently supported our silliness while enduring babbling about places and people who slowly came into existence through conversations, rewrites, and an abundance of sunflower seeds.

Three baseball lovers contributed guidance that shows up throughout these pages. Casey Andrews, Andrew Meny, and Chris Meny not only have strikingly similar names, they are full of stories and expertise.

Andrews McMeel Publishing
a division of Andrews McMeel Universal
1130 Walnut Street, Kansas City, Missouri 64106

www.andrewsmcmeel.com

24 25 26 27 28 SDB 10 9 8 7 6 5 4 3 2 1

Paperback ISBN: 978-1-5248-8479-6
Hardback ISBN: 978-1-5248-8489-5

Library of Congress Control Number: 2023947753

Made by:
RR Donnelley (Guangdong) Printing Solutions Company Ltd
Address and location of manufacturer:
No. 2, Minzhu Road, Daning, Humen Town,
Dongguan City, Guangdong Province, China 523930
1st Printing – 01/01/24

Editor: Erinn Pascal
Designer: Julie Barnes
Production Editor: Brianna Westervelt
Production Manager: Chuck Harper

ATTENTION: SCHOOLS AND BUSINESSES
Andrews McMeel books are available at quantity discounts with
bulk purchase for educational, business, or sales promotional use.
For information, please e-mail the Andrews McMeel Publishing
Special Sales Department: sales@amuniversal.com.